"See me out?" he asked, wondering if she'd oblige or hurl the carryout bag at his head.

When she stood and turned for the door, he smiled. He wondered how well her innately polite nature fared in the midst of her daily police duties.

Sophia had already pulled open the door, where she stood steeling herself against the desire to tap her bare foot.

Santigo took his time about approaching the door. Once he'd closed whatever distance there was between them, Sophia drew on every ounce of will not to throw herself on him again.

Tigo leaned into her, dipping his head to trail his nose across her temple, down her cheek…. Cupping her neck in his palm, he placed a lingering kiss on her earlobe.

"See you tomorrow."

"Tig…" Her tone was half needy, half tortured.

Santigo slid the kiss below her earlobe and then alongside her neck, and he felt her shudder.

Sophia had no more words. She could only turn her face toward him, where she breathed in the cologne he wore. The subtle fragrance triggered every hormone she claimed.

"Lock up." He spoke the order into the hollow at her throat. He straightened, taking delight in her reaction to his touch.

He gave her bottom a squeeze and proprietary pat, then he was gone. Sophia had just enough strength in her hand to set the locks before she had to rely on the door for support, as her legs had become totally useless.

Books by AlTonya Washington

Harlequin Kimani Romance

A Lover's Pretense
A Lover's Mask
Pride and Consequence
Rival's Desire
Hudson's Crossing
The Doctor's Private Visit
As Good as the First Time
Every Chance I Get
Private Melody
Pleasure After Hours
Texas Love Song
His Texas Touch
Provocative Territory
Provocative Passion

ALTONYA WASHINGTON

has been a romance novelist for nine years. Her novel *Finding Love Again* won the *RT Book Reviews* Reviewer's Choice Award for Best Multicultural Romance in 2004. As T. Onyx, AlTonya released her third erotica title, *Pleasure's Powerhouse*, in 2011. Her 2012 Harlequin Kimani Romance title *His Texas Touch*, second in the Lone Star Seduction series, was nominated for the *RT Book Reviews* Award in the Best Series Romance category. The year 2012 also marked the release of the fourteenth title in her popular Ramsey/Tesano saga, *A Lover's Sin*. The author began 2013 with her Harlequin Kimani Romance title *Provocative Territory*. She enjoys being a mom and librarian in North Carolina.

PROVOCATIVE
PASSION

ALTONYA WASHINGTON

⟨H⟩ **HARLEQUIN**®KIMANI™ROMANCE

To my incredible readers, friends and family. Your
awesome support continues to overwhelm me.

Recycling programs
for this product may
not exist in your area.

ISBN-13: 978-0-373-86315-0

PROVOCATIVE PASSION

HARLEQUIN®

Printed in U.S.A.   ™ www.Harlequin.com

Dear Reader,

Provocative Passion was a rare treat to craft. The experience was a mystery much like the one that unfolds among the pages you're about to read. Plotting this story and creating these alluring and very demanding characters was as much of a treat as it was a surprise.

I call the experience a mystery because I still can't quite figure out how these characters manage to dictate the course of the stories we authors create. It's amazing to be in the midst of drafting an outline and having a clear picture of the story's path, only to have it all redirected by the characters.

It's so exciting and motivating to still be surprised like this. Santigo Rodriguez, Sophia Hail and company definitely threw up tons of twists and turns in this book. I do hope you're ready for the ride.

Love and blessings,

Al

altonya@lovealtonya.com

Prologue

"Walk out that door and I'm done."

Sophia Hail's bow-shaped mouth opened in disbelief... and heartbreak. "You can't mean that." Her voice was less than a whisper.

The gold flecks in Santigo Rodriguez's uncommon ebony gaze sparkled; then his stare faltered and he was taking a seat in the armchair next to the bed, where he began slipping into a pair of black hiking boots.

"You mean that?" Sophia hated the lost and still-heartbroken tone of her voice. She was made of stronger stuff than that, but her disbelief had stunned her.

Santigo continued coolly putting on his shoes until the weight of Sophia's extraordinary gray eyes commanded a response. "How I feel shouldn't be a surprise, Soap," he said.

She shook her head. "All that time I've been at the academy—"

"And all that time you knew how I felt."

"Tig, it's my first day at work—"

"If it is, then I'm done."

Something flickered in her eyes, and she came to stand before him, arms folded over her chest. "You didn't think I'd go through with it, did you? Didn't think I'd finish." She saw the muscle skip along the angle of his strong jaw, and she knew she'd correctly guessed. "You jackass."

Santigo finished tying the boots and reclined in the chair. "You proved you have the stones to see this through. Let it go and move on."

Sophia placed the dry-cleaned uniform across her bed and pinned her lover of six years with a furious glare. "Move on? Why? To make it easier for *you* to handle?"

Tigo shot up from the chair, towering over Sophia and fixing her with a gaze darker than anything she could have conjured.

"Are you *that* ready to get yourself shot to hell to prove what a badass you are, Sophia?"

She took a step back…crushed. "That's what you think?" She took in the tall, seductively crafted length of his six-foot-plus frame. "When I told you this was who I am, who I wanted to be…did you think I was playing around, Tig?"

He spread his arms. "You wanna break me down, Soap? All right then, I admit it, I can't handle it." He shook his head; the generous curve of his mouth was a grim line. "I can't handle it."

"But you can handle me walking away from something *I* love?"

"Love? Jesus, Soap, you haven't even started!"

"Well, that's about to change." She went to reclaim her uniform.

"Then *we're* about to change." He turned his back and pulled a wrinkled denim shirt across his chiseled chestnut-brown torso.

Sophia bit her lip and willed herself not to cry. She

watched the uniform turn to a blur before her eyes and knew that she had failed.

"Leave my key on the counter when you go," she said and left without another look back.

Santigo maintained his rigid stance a mere second after the front door slammed shut. Then he crumpled, returning to the armchair, where he held his head in his hands and let emotion have its way.

Chapter 1

Sophia Hail was barely halfway through elementary school when her parents began Reed House. Gerald Hail, Sophia's father, was a well-known textile manufacturer. His factory put to work hundreds of people in and around the greater Philadelphia area.

Gerald's wife, Veronica, was a teacher in the same school her daughters Viva and Sophia attended. But Veronica was a dedicated daughter first and foremost. She was also an only child. When her parents grew ill, she left the career she treasured to care for them. For all her selflessness, Veronica pressed her girls to always follow their hearts. She urged them to seek and live their dreams for as long as their lives allowed them the option.

Sophia recalled her grandparents' illnesses all too well in spite of her age at the time. She also recalled her mother's heartbreak when Veronica realized how ill-equipped she was to care for them. Supportive to a fault, Gerald Hail had told his wife to spare no expense to find them the best.

The endeavor opened the Hails' eyes to the lack of quality care for the city's elderly. Once more, Veronica had found a passion—a new one that far surpassed her desire to teach. As she couldn't find quality care, she decided to create it herself for her parents and for other parents who, after a lifetime of caring for others, could no longer care for themselves.

Reed House, named for Veronica's parents, Glenn and Estelle Reed, grew into a premiere example of senior care. Local and national news stories had followed the assisted living center from its earliest days in a quaint Victorian-style home, capable of accommodating twenty "guests," to the impressive assisted living park, sprawled over a ten-acre tract of land just outside Philadelphia's city limits.

Veronica Hail was committed to providing her guests with virtually every aspect of the lives they'd enjoyed before the onset of age led them to her doors. Reed House was more than a retirement home. Nonresidents raved over the fine restaurants, which were exclusive to the center. It had often been said that Veronica Hail had discovered the secret to getting people to visit their loved ones in retirement homes more often: fine food.

Movie theaters, performance halls, an eighteen-hole golf course, community gardens…virtually any interest was indulged. The center earned its reputation as the finest example of elder care. There was certainly no shortage of funds to operate such an establishment, either. Veronica worked hard so that Reed House would be able to accept all applicants regardless of financial status.

The annual Reed House Jazz Supper was but one of the ways she made that possible. The supper had been a staple in Philadelphia for years. The award-winning entertainment flown in for the Jazz Supper often took a backseat to features on Reed House itself and the awesome work it accomplished. The acclaim was always abundant and consistent, and Reed House had managed to operate without scandal since its inception.

That had all changed seven days ago.

Sophia Hail didn't need to see or speak with her parents to know how disappointed they were by the events that had taken place during the Supper. Although a wrong had been righted, Sophia knew that her parents were more focused on *where* the wrong had been righted.

The arrest of Waymon Cole at the event still had the city reeling from all the revelations and backlash it had created.

Cole was a financier who was known best as business manager to Jazmina Beaumont, the owner of Jazzy B's Gentleman's Club. The woman's death had roused a power struggle of sorts between Cole and Jaz Beaumont's niece, Clarissa David. Waymon Cole wanted to maintain a stake in the club as it was his front for a complex money-laundering scheme that involved many of the city's "finest."

Sophia's work with Clarissa David had uncovered the crime and many of its participants. Sophia was especially determined to see the racket brought to an end in light of the nurturing role Jaz Beaumont had played in her sister Viva's life.

Unfortunately for Sophia, her dedication to seeing the case closed put her at odds with her parents. Once again, her job had aggravated the sore spot the Hails had harbored since their daughter had announced her desire to join the police force. Veronica Hail refused to believe that such an occupation could truly be her daughter's passion.

The closing of the case also put Sophia at odds with many of her coworkers. Given her line of work, such an upset could make for a dangerous situation.

That all took a backseat, however, to what weighed most heavily on her mind: the fact that she'd had to cancel her date with Santigo Rodriguez.

He'd taken her call to cancel quite well, as she remembered. Then again, he was probably used to it despite the fact that they hadn't dated in years. After all, it had been the demands of Sophia's job that had crippled their relationship in the first place.

Santigo's offer to take her to the Jazz Supper was most likely a fluke anyway. Sophia had been having lunch with Clarissa David. They had been discussing the case when Sophia had looked up and there he was. After eight years of not seeing each other once, there he was. Maybe he thought it meant something. They lived in the same city and hadn't run into each other at all before that day. Sophia had wondered if it'd meant anything, as well. She could barely hear herself accept his offer above the bass-drum beat of her heart in her ears.

She'd spoken to him only once since the Cole arrest. Even then, he'd sounded calm, telling her, "Work happens." He'd sounded cool enough, yet Sophia couldn't help but make note of the change in his demeanor. He'd made a joke about being too old to get riled up over things. Even still, Sophia remembered her ex-lover's temper all too well.

She had to wonder how long the slower-to-rile, easier-going Tigo Rodriguez would maintain a presence.

Sophia jerked herself from the cavern of her thoughts and found that the coffee she'd been nursing in the break room had grown cold. Settling back in the uncomfortable metal chair, she sighed. Her dark gray stare appeared as weary as she felt while she studied the clutter she'd made on the small round table she occupied.

She had taken to finishing reports and making calls in the area since the case had broken wide-open. The remote space was rarely used since most cops took to eating at their desks or heading out.

Sophia grimaced and traced the tip of an index nail around the coffee circle the bottom of her cup had left on the manila folder. Break time in a bona fide break area or at a desk would be forever changed when upward of twenty cops—soon to be former cops—would either be sent to the unemployment line or jail.

And that was all her doing. Many of Sophia's remaining coworkers blamed her for it all. This, regardless of the fact that the disgraced officers were dirty cops. It was a tough thing to deal with, tougher than it might have been, given the whole Reed House dinner fiasco.

Her colleagues had said little, but they didn't need to. Their thoughts were clearly echoed in the venomous looks they slithered her way. Sophia snorted, wrinkling a small nose spaced perfectly above her bow-shaped mouth. Being treated like an outsider was no surprise. She'd never received much more than a "hi" or "bye" from her coworkers anyway.

Because of who her parents were, almost everyone thought Sophia was merely *playing* cop. She couldn't blame them. There weren't too many heiresses who chose to be public servants.

A tap on her shoulder jerked Sophia from her thoughts for the second time that day.

"Sorry." Kelly Fields made the apology sound like a word of welcome as she smiled down at Sophia. "I've been looking all over for you."

Sophia winced and took in her surroundings. "Sorry about that." The apology was humble and genuine. Kelly was one of the switchboard operators, and that group rarely journeyed from the hallowed department that served as the nerve center of the precinct.

"Why didn't you call?" Sophia began to put the cluttered network of papers into some kind of order. "Oh," she said on discovering that her phone was nowhere on the small table or in the pockets she patted on her navy trousers.

Kelly cleared her throat, and Sophia looked up to find the petite redhead waving her cell phone lazily.

"I went by your office to look for you first," Kelly explained.

"Thanks." Sophia shook her head and took the phone.

"Not a problem."

"No, really." Sophia turned the rectangular device over in her hand. "Thanks for being thoughtful enough to drop this off. At least there's somebody around here who's not treating me like a pariah."

Kelly threw back her head and laughed. "I'm sure it's not as bad as you think."

"Hmph." Sophia toyed with a loose mahogany-brown curl she'd left dangling from her chignon. "What cop shop do *you* work for?"

"Well, the D.A.'s been trying to track you down," Kelly said after another bout of laughter. "She wants you to call her ASAP."

"Thanks again, Kelly." Sophia raised her phone in a gesture of mock salute.

Kelly leaned over to give Sophia's shoulder a reassuring squeeze. "Thank *you*."

Sophia smiled at the young woman's departing figure and then got to work returning the district attorney's call.

D.A. Paula Starker rarely answered a call with a hello. There were always the few additional moments it took for her to close out the conversation she was already involved in before she gave the next person her full attention.

Sophia smiled and listened in as Paula spoke to who Sophia assumed was one of her assistants.

"Now find me at least one piece of worthwhile evidence we can take into court instead of the beef the defense ground the prosecution's ass into yesterday. Hello?" Paula answered the call as though it was an afterthought.

"Returning your call, Madam D.A.," Sophia sang.

"Ah…Detective Sophia, don't you own a mobile? I've been trying to reach you all morning. Waymon Cole?" The clipped,

no-nonsense tone Paula reserved for her A.D.A.s had softened into her more natural native Georgia drawl.

"Cole." Sophia frowned. "What about him?"

"Wants a deal."

"Impossible."

"Possible. That is, if what he's dealing is good."

Sophia left the small table and began to stalk the uninviting, fluorescent-lit room. "What's he dealing?" Her voice
was like stone.

"I'd rather discuss that in person. When can you meet
me?"

Sophia was preparing to reply when the phone shook with
another call coming through. Santigo.

"Paula, um, let me get back to you. Another call's coming in."

"Not a problem. I'll look to hear from you before five."

"Right." Sophia made quick work of clicking off from
Paula to catch Tigo's call before it went to voice mail. Still,
she took care not to sound overly excited when she greeted
him.

"Hey, Tig."

"Hey." His voice was like caramel over chipped ice—
sweet, cool and with an edge that roused shivers that had
nothing to do with a chill. "This a bad time?" he asked.

"No, no, not a bit."

"You're lying." He sounded amused. "But I won't hold it
against you. I want you for dinner."

"Do *I* get to eat, too?" *Hell. Where did that come from?*
Sophia asked herself. The words had tumbled past her lips so
fast she hadn't even realized they'd been verbalized.

Santigo laughed, the sound warm and thick. Obviously,
he was surprised by her comeback. "Sure you do, but I get
the feeling you don't eat much."

"So is this your way of saving me?" Sophia returned to
settle back into the hard metal chair.

"Trying to save myself, Soap." The caramel smoothness went soft, quietly affecting. "I'll see you soon, all right?"

He disconnected before Sophia could say anything else. She studied the phone, rolling it over in her hand. "Do you know what you're doing, girl? Uh-uh," she answered herself in the negative. She never knew what she was doing when it came to Santigo Rodriguez.

"Oh, hey, Sophia!" Dionne Battles, another of the switchboard crew, strolled into the break room on stylish six-inch heels. "D.A. Starker's been tryin' to reach you."

"Thanks, Dee." Sophia threw a hand up to the operator who was on the way to the candy machine in the corner of the dim room. Turning back to the papers in her hand, she told herself to get back to work—the only thing she did well.

Santigo Rodriguez and his partner Linus Brooks were trading amused looks as they subjected their partner and old friend Elias Joss to a series of twenty or more questions. Elias had just announced that he was taking a quick trip, and he stood behind his desk trying to convince his partners that it was all business.

"Ah, man, please. You need to squash that," Linus grunted with a playful smirk.

Tigo chuckled. "Line's right, El. Admit it. Business and Clarissa David don't even belong in the same paragraph for you."

Eli kept his gaze on the folder he held. "We're professionals," he said.

"Bull," Tigo declared.

"Double bull," Linus added in the same playful grunt he'd used earlier.

Elias rolled his eyes, two mesmerizing orbs of sky blue that contrasted against a complexion of creamy caramel. "I seem to recall all of us being in the same meeting, where we decided to visit the locales of the clubs." Joss Construction had won the bid for the redesign of Jazzy B's locations across the country. Clarissa and Elias were to set off on a series of trips meant to ensure Clarissa's desires for the clubs were along the same lines as the architects' working with Joss.

"Damn." Santigo closed his eyes and raked both hands through the silky coal-colored waves crowning his head. "Line, man, help me out. What's the word I'm lookin' for?"

"Convenient," Linus supplied, idly scanning the copy of *Architectural Digest* he'd grabbed from an end table.

"That's it." Tigo snapped his fingers.

Eli grimaced, but it was all in fun. "I'm thinking of a word, too." He shut the folder he'd been attempting to browse. "Maybe two words—*peaceful* and *quiet.*"

"Ah, man." Tigo threw up a lazy wave. "Don't get upset because you can't admit you're using business to fulfill your pleasure."

Elias tried to appear exasperated but only broke down in amusement. Soon all three men were enjoying a hearty round of laughter.

"Seriously, El." Linus stood once the largest portion of laughter had been spent. "You and Clarissa, it's a good look." He slanted his friend a wink.

Elias reciprocated with a nod. "Doesn't feel half-bad, either," he confessed.

Linus walked over to shake hands with Eli, and then he took his suit coat from the back of the armchair he'd occupied and left the office.

Tigo left his place on the sofa and strolled the room to claim a new spot on the edge of Elias's desk. "He's right," Tigo said.

Elias gave his friend the benefit of a quick and knowing smile before resuming his scan of the folder's contents. "Think you're in line for the same?"

"Huh?" Tigo's hand stilled on the paperweight on the desk. He laughed abruptly at the look Elias sent his way.

"Don't even try it." Eli closed the folder and picked up another. "We all know you've seen Sophia. Even Clari could tell there was something up when she saw the way you were drooling over her when they had lunch that day."

"Ain't that cute? You and Clarissa already exchanging scoops about mutual friends. This *is* serious." Tigo bounced the weight in his palm.

"All right, all right." Elias laughed. "Keep your secrets."

A few moments passed with only the sound of Eli sorting through folders dotting the silence.

"I want her back." Santigo eased the chrome paperweight back to its stand on the desk. "I don't plan to let her walk away from me again."

"Hmm…*let* her walk away. Don't you mean you don't plan to *tell* her to walk away?"

"Don't start, El," Tigo warned through a clenched jaw.

Elias kept his gaze on the open folder. "This won't work if you can't be honest about why it didn't work out in the first place." He looked at Santigo. "You're gonna have to own up to the ultimatum you gave her. You can best believe she hasn't forgotten it. And last I heard, she was still a cop."

"Right." Tigo acknowledged the fact in a deep voice as tight as his clenched jaw.

"And that still bothers you," Eli guessed. He took his suit coat from the rack in the corner.

"So what? It bothers me." Tigo jerked his shirt cuffs with more force than was needed. "It doesn't mean I can't have her."

"No…it doesn't mean that." Eli slipped an arm into the amber-colored jacket. "But if it bothers you the way it did before, you should ready yourself for the sight of her walking away from you again." Elias finished donning the coat and grabbed the folders he'd been studying. He paused to pat Santigo's cheek before making his way out of the office.

* * *

"All right, now we're on the right track. *This* is evidence." Paula Starker was speaking to one of her A.D.A.s while nodding enthusiastically at the thick file she browsed. "It's got gums, but you still need something with teeth... Detective Sophie!" she greeted in the same breath when she looked around.

"Bring me something juicy, Rich," Paula told the harried-looking young man. She handed him the file and waved him off, grinning at Sophia as the A.D.A. rushed out.

"Something juicy?" Sophia shook her head. "I'll bet he's got all kinds of ideas running through his head."

"Ha! So long as he keeps 'em there, we're good, Detective Sophie." Paula tossed a pen on the desk teeming with heavy-bound books, legal pads and folders.

Sophia took a seat on the arm of the tan leather sofa nearby. "You know, I really don't think your greeting me as Detective Sophie is professional, *Pauly*."

"Ahh..." Paula waved off the caution. "Do you really think folks don't already know we went to school together and were roommates besides?"

Paula Starker was new to her post as D.A. The fact that a woman in her mid-thirties had unseated the former holder of the seat after a ten-year term was almost as startling as the fact that she was a black.

Sophia left the sofa, rubbing chilled hands as she headed for the coffee carafe set out near the liquor shelf in Paula's office. "It might be an issue if we keep meeting this way. You say Cole wants to deal?"

"Says he's got deal-worthy information. Funny how an arraignment not going your way will do that. Judge denied bail." She shrugged. "For now."

Sophia inhaled the coffee's aroma as she poured it into a large mug. "So what's this deal-worthy info?"

Paula waved her mug in a silent request for Sophia to provide a refill of the fragrant walnut blend. "He's being tight-lipped. Understandable. But it doesn't take a genius to figure what he's bartering."

Sophia filled Paula's mug and returned it. "He wants to name names," she guessed.

"I'll say." Paula took a timid sip of the brew. "Obviously he and Paul Hertz are on the B-list."

Sophia added cream to her coffee, frowning over Paula's mention of Paul Hertz, who had submitted his resignation as chief of detectives following his arrest along with several other uniforms who had been tracked by their badge numbers from a ledger belonging to Waymon Cole. The ledger had been discovered by Clarissa David among her late aunt's belongings.

"We took down a lot of people, Pauly. That's nothin' to sneeze at."

"Cops and a glorified stockbroker." Paula set aside the coffee as though she'd lost her taste for it. "Do you really believe Cole and Hertz are as far up the food chain as this thing goes?" A measure of confidence faded from the woman's round, honey-toned face. "If Cole does have something, I can't make a deal for it. I could kiss off any chance for keeping my job if I did. We've gotta find Cole's goodies without his help."

Sophia hissed an indecipherable curse. "I just hoped all this was—"

"What? Over?" Paula recrossed her shapely legs beneath her side-split rose-blush skirt. "Guess you thought all the bad guys were behind bars?"

Sophia smiled in spite of herself. "Yeah…naive, I know, and a little anxious, I guess…."

"Anxious, huh?" Paula's champagne-colored stare sparkled with a bit of wickedness. "Could that have anything to do with a certain half-black, half-Hispanic brotha, initials S.R.?"

The surprise on Sophia's dark face sent Paula chuckling. "I heard he came to see you at the station. Ha! We're a pair, aren't we? Both of us could use more friends in our places of business. You've probably got more pull around here than I do, and *I've* probably got a bit more at the precinct that *you* do."

"It was nothing to throw a parade over." Sophia warmed her hands around the mug and remembered the day Tigo had come by the station. "The visit didn't even last five minutes."

"And you were okay with that?" Paula sat behind her desk.

Sophia laughed. "There was nothing to be okay with. Anyway." She folded her arms across the gray blouse beneath her jacket. "Where should we start tryin' to dig up the rest of Cole's secrets?"

"And this is where more friends would come in handy." Paula toyed with a curl from her bob. "You should have as little involvement in this part of the investigation as possible. Put some other bodies on this. Offer guidance but only at a distance. If you didn't have any friends at the station before, then you've got even less now."

Sophia looked like she'd just been slapped. "Paula, are you stupid? How can you lay something like this at my feet and not expect me to get involved?"

"Listen to me, So-So. If what I've heard is true, you'll soon be in a position to delegate having somebody to do everything short of wiping your nose for you. Just keep a low profile on this." She scratched her temple and grimaced. "The curtains are being pulled off a lot of shady windows in this city. Things may get a lot worse before they get any better, so you just be careful, Detective. We can't afford to lose any more good cops."

The easy glow returned to Paula's face and she reached for her coffee mug. "You just delegate and chill out. I'm sure you can find finer ways to spend your time and with finer people. *Initials S.R.*," she sang.

Sophia smiled, unable and unwilling to discuss the shiver that danced up her spine.

Chapter 2

Sophia rushed home right after her shift. It was something she rarely did. There was always one more thing to be done—one last report to file, one more lead to follow. That was before Santigo Rodriguez had resumed his place at the top of her thoughts.

She showered, changed and, so as not to appear completely desperate for his company, entertained herself by reading up on the notes she had from the Waymon Cole case. She scoured the pages for anything that might offer a lead to the food chain Paula had alluded to.

Her mind wasn't on it, though. The words were practically blurring together on the pages. *Damn it!* she thought, suddenly resenting Tigo's reappearance in her life.

She was just getting used to getting along without him. Wasn't she? Sophia couldn't or wouldn't answer the question. Just as well since her doorbell was ringing. Quickly, she brushed her hands across the seat of her shorts and went to answer the door.

Tigo's glare held the unmistakable tint of amusement. "A cop shouldn't be so careless. You didn't even ask who it was."

Sophia tossed her head, sending her high ponytail swinging playfully. "I've got a gun," she reminded him.

He bowed his head, nodding while he leaned on the door frame. "What if he didn't give you time to pull it?"

Sophia bit her lip, happily willing to melt in response to the alluring depth of his voice. "I do have other ways of defending myself." She almost didn't recognize the breathy tinge to her words.

Tigo pushed off the jamb. "And what if he did something you couldn't defend against?"

Her gray stare was fixed on his mouth. "Like what?" At that point she didn't care how breathless she was.

Santigo didn't disappoint. He'd barely dipped his head to oblige her unspoken plea when Sophia moved to her toes and eagerly drew him to her.

One of them moaned. Tigo rested his lean, athletic frame against the door, still holding her securely to him. Sophia savored the lunges of his tongue in her mouth and met the powerful drives of it against hers with her own thrusts of equal intensity, equal need.

She moaned, that time clearly recognizing the gesture as her own. She locked her arms around his neck, wantonly rubbing her body against his, needing to feel every inch of him.

"Sophie." His whisper sounded suspiciously like a whimper. He curved one hand around her bottom, his thumb grazing the hint of cheek visible beneath the frayed hem of her cutoffs. "Babe?" he murmured amid the lusty thrusting of their tongues.

"Hmm…" Sophia had sealed herself against him so that not one ounce of space existed between them.

"Soap," he growled his pet name for her and squeezed her bottom with a bit more insistence.

Sophia shivered from the sound of the endearment that

she hadn't heard in so long. It was then that she heard the rustling emerging from below and realized that Tigo was tugging her back. She blinked, taking stock of her actions and the burning sensation in her cheeks.

"I promised dinner," he said and gave the bag he held another shake.

Sophia hadn't even noticed it before, and she could not have cared less whether or not he'd kept that particular promise. She wasn't hungry for food. Still, she recognized the logic in exercising a little more…restraint.

"Right." She turned away to indulge in a few deep breaths and the necessary lash fluttering while she composed herself. "Do we need plates?"

Tigo shook the bag and moved off the door. "Only if you have a problem eating out of the box."

Sophia whirled, observing the bag with more interest. "Chinese?"

"Uh-huh." The striking length of his sleek brows merged to form a frown. "You still eat it, don't you?"

"Don't be stupid."

He laughed and moved farther into her cozy apartment. "Where would you like to have it?"

Sophia could have swooned then for sure. Chinese food in bed, before and after sex, had been one of their many indulgences during the course of their very passionate relationship. Whatever differences they may've had outside the bedroom carried no power inside it.

Tigo waited patiently for Sophia's response, knowing exactly what was going through her mind. It'd been going through his mind all day, longer…. He took stock of her attire. She wore a simple ensemble consisting of a throwback Eagles jersey that virtually covered the denim cutoffs beneath it.

Simple attire or not, it gave him all kinds of ideas and returned all sorts of memories.

"We can eat right in here." Sophia threw a loose wave toward the living room. "At the coffee table." Overrun by memories, as well, she knew she was doing a poor job of hiding her fluster.

They studied each other. One quietly observing the other. Just as her eyes had lingered on his mouth, Sophia was fixated on the gold chain he wore, just visible below the open collar of his burgundy shirt. The tails hung outside the waist of his black trousers. Jewelry had always seemed out of place on other men in Sophia's opinion. On Tigo, it was just right. The piece had belonged to his father, who had died of a heart attack the summer before Tigo had started middle school.

"Would you, um…like a beer?" She asked once her unhurried perusal of his body had concluded.

"I'd like a lot of things, Soap." He turned away then to give her time to absorb his meaning. "But I'll settle for a beer." He started setting out the dinner.

"Why'd you call me after all this time, Tig?" Sophia queried in a soft, careful manner. They'd eaten in a surprisingly comfortable silence for almost thirty minutes. "I couldn't have looked *that* good the day you saw me at lunch with Clarissa," she murmured into her pint of shrimp lo mein.

Santigo smirked from his reclining position on the large navy armchair that flanked the sofa. "You have no idea," he replied.

"So what?" She looked up to meet his eyes, unmistakable challenge enhancing her dark lovely face. "Is this about ringing up an ex-lover for another go? Ah…there it is." She caught sight of the jaw muscle he clenched. "I was wondering if you still had that temper." She snuggled into the sofa, intent on capturing one of the plump shrimp amid the noodles.

"Yeah, I've still got the temper, Sophie. Stupidity always brings it out in me."

Sophia caught the shrimp and popped the morsel into her

mouth. "Stupidity? Hmph, I thought I was being very perceptive." She managed to sound cool enough when it was all she could do to chew her food as she weighed his reaction.

When there was no reaction, she returned her flint-colored gaze to the pint of food. "Why did you call me, Tig?" she whispered.

"I miss you. I miss you in every way." There was no hesitation in his response.

Sophia worked the chopsticks deeper into the box and smiled. "So this *was* about calling me up for another go?"

"Is that why you answered?" he countered.

"Of course not." She cleared her throat on the lie.

What else could she say, though? That she hadn't had sex with anyone since him? That on more occasions than she cared to admit, she could only fall asleep after pleasuring herself using memories of them together for stimulus?

She observed him covertly through the thickness of her lashes. He was a picture of ease. She'd be a fool to say he didn't affect her. What woman wouldn't be affected by him? His features were a perfect mesh of his biracial heritage, compliments of his African-American mother and Puerto Rican father. His eyes even carried traces of both parents. The gold flecks were a testament to his mother's rich hazel gaze. They sparkled amid a sea of bottomless ebony, compliments of his father. The fierce perfection of his features was softened by the easy humor that lurked in his stare.

What woman wouldn't mind being the target of his attention? Sophia asked herself again. He'd always been able to gauge the tracks of her thoughts using little effort, and she resented him for it.

In spite of their years together, she had never been able to get a line on his innermost thoughts. The fact that she was a cop and pretty good at getting into other people's heads made acknowledging her failure at reading Tigo's mind a difficult thing to admit.

Then again, she wasn't a cop around Santigo Rodriguez, was she? She was a woman, just a woman who craved the man who sat in her living room acting like he had no idea what he did to her.

"Thanks for dinner, Tig." She uncrossed her legs and scooted forward to gather empty and nearly empty containers. "It's been a long time since I enjoyed Chinese *with* someone." She returned the items to the carryout bag.

Tigo wondered how often she enjoyed food at all. He knew that she had a tendency to forgo eating when she was in the middle of a project. Years ago, work had consisted of school. Now, it consisted of crime solving and saving lives. Yes, he had a fine idea of how often and how well she ate.

Thankfully, the bad habit hadn't taken a negative toll on the shapeliness of her tall, mahogany-brown frame. Every part of him roared that he was a pure idiot for denying her when she was all but handing herself to him on a platter.

She hadn't changed. Correction, she had changed in the most beautifully subtle ways he could imagine. She'd always been tall, but her very slender frame had acquired an alluring set of curves honed by her very active lifestyle. The bow-shaped mouth and tiny nose still gave her the doll-like appearance that clashed provocatively with the dark gray, almond-shaped eyes. His fingers literally ached to lose themselves in the loose shoulder-length curls that were as mahogany-rich as her skin.

"I should go." He muttered the phrase "pure idiot" below his breath as soon as he heard the words leave his tongue.

"Yeah, you probably should." Sophia was shoving used napkins and utensils into the bag.

"See me out?" he asked, wondering if she'd oblige or hurl the carryout bag at his head. When she stood and turned for the door, he smiled. He wondered how well her innately polite nature fared in the midst of her daily police duties.

Sophia had already pulled open the door and stood steeling herself against the desire to tap her bare foot.

Santigo took his time about approaching the door. Once he'd closed whatever distance there was between them, Sophia drew on every ounce of will not to throw herself on him again.

Tigo leaned into her, dipping his head to trail his nose across her temple, down her cheek… Cuffing her neck in his palm, he placed a lingering kiss on her earlobe.

"See you tomorrow."

"Tig…" Her tone was half needy, half tortured.

Santigo slid the kiss below her earlobe and then alongside her neck, and he felt her shudder.

Sophia had no more words. She could only turn her face toward him, where she breathed in the cologne he wore. The subtle fragrance triggered every hormone she claimed.

"Lock up." He spoke the order into the hollow at her throat. He straightened, taking delight in her reaction to his touch.

He gave her bottom a squeeze and proprietary pat; then he was gone. Sophia had just enough strength in her hand to set the locks before she had to rely on the door for support—her legs had become totally useless.

Linus Brooks was used to being the more wary head between his two partners. Elias was usually immovable, with the ability to make precise decisions based on the facts at hand. Santigo used his capacity for calm and easygoingness to give people enough rope to hang themselves. It was his method of separating trash from treasure.

Linus felt he'd crafted the art of seeing folks for what they were right off the bat. Therefore, he took great enjoyment in taking the lead during meetings.

That morning, his joy was overshadowed by Santigo's obvious mood. Linus found himself letting the architects on one of their latest projects off the hook a bit more easily as he was anxious to discover what was up with his friend.

"Spill it," Linus ordered once the architects had beat a hasty path for the conference room door.

Tigo was still gathering his thoughts when he heard his partner. He frowned, noticing Linus's liquid brown eyes on him. "What?"

"What's up with the mood? I'm supposed to be the brooding one."

Linus's playfully put-out tone brought an unwilling grin to Tigo's face. After a few seconds of debate, he set the tablet and mobile on the table and then loosened the olive-green tie from his collar.

"Saw Sophia last night."

Linus whistled. "Now *that's* a name from the past."

"Yeah…" Tigo worked the bunched muscles at his neck once he'd loosened the top buttons of his shirt. "I saw her having lunch with Clarissa a while back. Soap was helping her get to the bottom of that mess with her aunt's clubs."

"So next you're calling her and then…what?" Linus reared back in the black swivel chair and crossed his feet atop the long rectangular table. "Will you be next to head off on a 'business' trip?" He curved his index and middle fingers to quote the word.

Tigo chuckled, recognizing the dig at Elias's trip with Clarissa. "We're not there yet. Far from it." He sighed.

"Ah…" Linus grinned and folded his hands in his lap. "Detective Hail's gonna make you work for it, huh?"

"Hmm…" Tigo scratched his eyebrow and took a seat on the edge of the table. "It's not her. *I'm* the one who wants to…work for it."

"Say what?" Linus almost laughed the words while he pulled his feet off the table and leaned forward.

Tigo nudged his fingers against the tablet's leather casing.

"She was willing, but I, um, I just want us to start off better than that, you know?"

"What the hell are you talkin' about, T?"

Santigo muttered something vile, cursing that he'd confided too much. Unfortunately, it was too late to clam up then.

"I want us to wait before we have sex, all right?"

Linus dissolved into a lengthy bout of laughter. "Aw, man, that's sweet," he managed after a full minute.

"See? That's why I always talk to Eli." Tigo waved off Linus. "It's impossible to talk serious to you."

"Hold up, man." Linus wiped tears from the corners of his eyes and stifled what remained of the laughter. "You already took her virginity a long time ago, right?"

Tigo merely shook his head and began taking his things from the table.

"Tigo, wait—"

"Save it." .

"Seriously, man." Linus extended a hand across the table. "I'm sorry, seriously." He waited for Tigo to put down his belongings. "It's just…is this a good idea? I mean, after what happened last time?"

"I remember. Damn." Tigo pushed a hand through his hair and returned to sit on the edge of the table.

"I want to make it right with her, Line. I never should've made her choose between me and her job."

Linus came to sit next to Tigo on the table. "You think her choice would be any different this time around?"

"I don't want to know what her choice would be." Tigo folded his arms over his double-breasted heather-brown suit coat. "I don't want her to make one. I only want her to make room for me. For us."

"So you're ready to accept that?" Linus folded his hands over the table's edge and studied his black loafers. "She's a real cop, you know? She's got no qualms about bein' in the line of fire. The girl's no desk-rider."

"I want her back, Line."

Linus nodded, knowing his friend well enough to know the matter was settled for him. "So how do you plan to make it happen?"

Tigo groaned. "Not a damn clue." He buried his face in his hands.

Linus massaged satiny facial whiskers, which had been tamed into a permanent five-o'clock shadow. Again he nodded. "But you know it involves denying what you both really want?"

"What I really want is her back."

"Bull. What you really want is her back eventually and her in your bed *now*."

Tigo grimaced, but his gaze was soft when he slanted a look at his friend. "I'm beginning to understand why you're single."

Linus slid off the table and shrugged. "She still got that doll face?"

Tigo bowed his head and massaged his neck again. "Yeah." He smiled, envisioning the woman he loved.

"Goddess body?" Linus inquired.

"Better than ever."

"Hell…" Linus's smoky, calculating stare was filtered with something wicked. "And you expect to woo her or whatever the devil your plan is without the thought of taking her to bed ever crossing your mind?"

A growl worked its way up Tigo's throat. "Hell, Line, that's the *only* thing on my mind."

"Exactly my point. Neither of you is gonna be able to focus on a damn thing with all that tension between you."

Tigo gave a wan smile. "Thanks for your support."

"I'm only saying that the situation is already stressful enough given your history." Linus inclined his head. "Why make it worse?" he asked.

Tigo considered Linus's point of view while taking a slow

stroll around the golden-lit conference room. "The way she looked at me last night when I tried to talk to her…maybe sex *is* all she's interested in." He worked the bridge of his nose between his thumb and index finger. "If we take it there, Line, and that's all she wants or expects from me…I'll never get anywhere with her."

Linus appeared as though he at least understood his friend's point of view. "You really do still love her, don't you?"

"Yeah…" Tigo massaged all ten fingers into his neck and smiled. "Yeah, I really still do."

"Captain. Chief," Sophia greeted Captain Roy Poltice and Chief of Police Dean Franklin. A surprised frown claimed her expression when she spotted the other unexpected face at the table. "Commissioner Meeks," she whispered and then cleared her throat as she extended a hand.

Police Commissioner Ethan Meeks was a sturdy, broadly built sixty-something man with a head full of snow-white hair that framed his face, which was usually brightened by a smile.

"Detective." Commissioner Meeks moved to envelop one of Sophia's slender hands in both of his beefy red ones. "We hope you've saved room for a big breakfast?"

"Have a seat, Sophia," Captain Poltice urged, expertly reading the young detective's stunned expression.

"We know you weren't expecting this particular cast of characters, Detective," Chief Franklin conceded once orders for coffee had been taken to the kitchen of the corner bistro where the meeting was taking place.

In truth, Sophia had only received the call about the gathering the night before, after her dinner with Santigo.

"Um, no, not at all, Chief." She remembered that she hadn't answered the man's question.

Her pitiful denial roused laughter from the three men.

Chief Franklin's dazzling white smile was a sharp, attractive contrast against his molasses-dark skin, and it had a quality that settled some of the nerves in Sophia's stomach.

"I thought I'd only be having breakfast with the captain." Sophia smoothed damp palms across her sandalwood-colored slacks. "Is anything wrong?"

"There is nothing wrong, Detective," Chief Franklin assured her. "In fact, it appears that things are finally on their way to being right again."

"Sir?" Sophia didn't mind letting her confusion show.

The query wasn't addressed until the waitress had arrived with the coffees and left with four hearty breakfast orders for bacon, hash browns, eggs and toast.

"Detective, we'd like to start by complimenting your work on the Cole case." Captain Poltice leaned forward and nodded in Sophia's direction. "You showed cool professionalism in what is still a very delicate situation."

"You knew the risk, knew the beehive you were about to aggravate, and still you moved forward," Chief Franklin added.

"With all due respect, sir." Sophia scooted forward in her chair. "I'm no statement maker or politician. I was just doing my job."

"Precisely, and that's why we can't think of a better detective for the job."

"Sir?" Sophia eyed the commissioner, who had spoken.

Commissioner Meeks's inviting smile came through again. "We're sure you've heard that Detective Hertz submitted his resignation. We've accepted it and would like to offer you the chief of detectives post. Will you accept it?"

Sophia ordered her brain to send word to her face that it wasn't polite to sit with one's mouth hanging open when meeting with the commissioner of the force. Her brain and her face didn't appear to be on speaking terms just then, however.

"I, um… This is… I…"

"Perhaps a couple of days to think it over might help?"

Sophia nodded gratefully at Chief Franklin's suggestion. "We'll give you forty-eight hours to get used to the idea."

"Right." Sophia pursed her lips at Captain Poltice's clarification of the chief's suggestion. The man's phrasing translated into: "The job's yours. Get used to it."

"You were at the top of a very short list, Detective. Actually, you were the list," the commissioner shared.

Sophia reached for her coffee, gulped it down and tried to smother a cough as the bitter black brew burned a path down her gullet. Though rattled by the effect, she had at least regained a firmer grasp on her verbal skills.

"Sirs, uh…previous chiefs of Ds…they haven't been posted until they were almost fifty. I'm barely into my thirties and…well, I am almost single-handedly responsible for my successor losing his job. That won't exactly instill a sense of welcome from my new staff."

"Perhaps not at first, Detective." Chief Franklin sipped at his coffee. "But one thing it *will* instill from the onset is a sense of decorum. It'll go without saying that you'll accept no half-assed work, cutting corners or shady measures. Cops under your command will know they play aboveboard or they don't play at all."

Sophia nudged her fingers against the handle of the gleaming silverware at her place setting. "What about the cops who think they can get away with it?"

The men traded looks.

"We know Paul Hertz wasn't at the top of this thing, Sophia," Roy Poltice said matter-of-factly. "Our new D.A. is on a mission to weed out every bad seed she can find. If she hadn't made contact with you about it yet, she will soon."

Commissioner Meeks set his coffee on the saucer with a slight clatter. "We know there're more rats to be shaken out of this blanket, Detective. When it's all said and done, we want to be able to show that we're taking this seriously and that we're determined to give the force a clean face again."

"So this is all for appearance sake?" Sophia asked.

"This is about initiative." Chief Franklin nodded to Captain Poltice. "We're all in agreement about the fine way you took charge and followed your instincts in getting to the bottom of an injustice.

"And you got results besides," the chief continued. "You followed every aspect of the case to the letter. Cole's and Hertz's attorneys will be hard-pressed to find any improprieties within the investigation.

"Using information we've yet to uncover to strike a deal for a lesser sentence is the only leverage they could possibly have. We'd like to take that away from them." Chief Franklin stirred his black coffee. "Take the forty-eight hours, Detective. Get used to the idea and give us the official call so we can give the media something else to salivate over."

The breakfast platters arrived, and, after a momentary clatter of plates next to mugs as they were set on the table, the group prepared to dive in.

Sophia watched as the three heavyset men showered their food with salt before they'd even tasted it. "I have just one more question," she said after eating heartily for several minutes.

"Anything, Detective." Captain Poltice added butter to his hash browns.

Sophia washed down eggs and toast with a swig of coffee. "As chief of detectives, will I have the chance to take part in the occasional bust?"

Silence hovered over the table until Roy Poltice's healthy frame began to shake. In seconds, all three of the high-ranking officers were deep in the clutches of ribald laughter. Sophia joined in moments later.

Chapter 3

Santigo's conversation with Linus following their meeting with the architects went on for a while longer and ended with drinks in Linus's office. Neither man wanted to admit that it was far too early in the day to be breaking the seal on a bottle of bourbon, but Tigo appreciated that Linus understood his trying predicament.

The partners indulged lightly but joyfully until Tigo remembered he had another meeting to attend. Linus was very persuasive, but Tigo admirably refused another round of the fine liquor.

"Carl and Lester are already inside," Jenny Boyce's childlike voice chirped out the information when Tigo arrived in the private lobby outside his office.

Tigo checked the platinum timepiece around his wrist. "They been waiting long?" he asked his assistant.

"Not more than five minutes." Jenny moved from behind her desk to help her boss straighten his tie. "They don't look so good." She spoke in a hushed tone.

That was news indeed since the two crew chiefs were known for their comedic wit and easy smiles. As Tigo's main responsibilities put him in contact with union reps and oftentimes tense negotiations, working with a laid-back duo like Carl and Lester was one of the few joys his job provided.

"Thanks, Jen." Tigo smoothed down the attractive olive-green tie with its subtle markings and cleared his throat while pushing open the double doors to his office.

"Gentlemen," he called out to Carl Roche and Lester Bradford. He made his way across the wide expanse of the room to shake hands with the two men, who waited before the gargantuan desk in the rear.

"Coffee? Somethin' stronger?" Tigo offered.

"Nah, thanks, T."

It didn't take much more than those few words from Carl for Tigo to share Jenny's assessment of the men's moods. "Is there trouble brewing in the ranks?" he asked.

"This isn't union business," Carl said.

"It's personal," Lester tacked on.

Tigo shrugged off his jacket and loosened his tie. "Talk to me," he offered in the blunt, inviting and informal manner all Joss Construction employees had come to love about him.

"You remember my boy Kenny?" Lester asked as he, Tigo and Carl took seats.

Tigo smiled, nodding from his perch at the edge of his desk. "How is he?"

"Working." Lester's smile hinged between pride and something akin to sorrow. "Last year in high school. He's working for Greenway Construction."

"Ugh." Tigo twisted his face into a playful frown. "Working for the enemy, huh?"

"Hmph, in more ways than one."

Tigo's amusement transitioned quickly into agitation. "What's goin' on, Les?"

Lester braced his elbows on the knees of his khaki work

pants and smoothed a hand back over his dark, balding head. "Some weeks back, Ken went to Carl's son, Ian, about makin' some extra money."

"Right." Tigo nodded, knowing that Ian Roche was one of their part-time crew members. "We don't own him, fellas. Ian's free to work with another company if he wants to."

"That ain't the problem, T." Carl Roche's face was a bit flushed beneath his honey-toned complexion. "The extra money wasn't from a construction job, but some…errand, and both the boys are sittin' downtown right now in a cell on a carjacking charge."

Tigo blinked—stunned. He knew the kids had taken work to earn extra money for college. To help their parents, both boys had agreed to start school a year later in order for their folks to get better prepared before they were hit with the expense.

"What can I do?" Tigo leaned forward, shifting his gaze between the two men.

The worried fathers traded uncertain looks. "We were hoping you could tell *us,* T." Carl Roche sighed.

"The public defenders on the boys' case are useless." Lester slumped back in his chair. "Judge says he wants to make an example of 'em."

"They haven't been in trouble before, have they?"

The fathers shook their heads in unison.

"So what possessed 'em to do somethin' so knuckle-headed?"

"The boys swear they didn't know a damn thing about the truck being stolen," Lester insisted.

"So how did this go down?" Santigo left his desk and assumed his place behind it. "Did they get pulled?"

Lester nodded. "Cops say it was a *routine* stop."

Carl grunted an ill-humored laugh. "Yeah, I guess even in the twenty-first century, two young black men driving around town in the wee hours of the morning still looks suspicious."

"Cops ran the plates. Truck came up stolen." Lester massaged the bridge of his nose.

"Hell…" Tigo ran a hand across his cheek while shaking his head. "What do the guys have to say?"

"Claim they were set up or some mess…."

Tigo frowned and looked to Carl for more clarification.

The man shrugged. "It's all we can get out of 'em right now."

"We just want our boys out of jail. Judge won't even budge on it."

"Who's the judge?" Tigo frowned at Lester.

The man said something foul below his breath. "Some fool…Oswald Stowe."

Tigo nodded, assessing the information. "Anything else I need to know? Have the boys given up a reason *why* they think they were set up?"

Carl let out another grunt. "Took us forever to get *that* much information out of them."

"All right then." Tigo pushed out of the wide gray suede swivel chair. "Don't you guys worry too much over this. I'll see what I can do." He rounded the desk to shake hands with both men and then muttered a curse of regret once the disillusioned fathers had dragged themselves from the office.

Sophia lingered behind the wheel of the car for a bit longer than she needed to. She had parked in the curving brick drive outside her parents' home and spent time running shaking hands through her hair once she'd unbound the professional updo she'd worn for the meeting with her superiors that morning.

She hadn't seen or spoken to her parents since shortly after Waymon Cole's arrest at the Reed House dinner. Even then, the conversation had been brief. It was long enough to tell Sophia that her mother and father clearly disapproved of the entire situation. More importantly, they disapproved of their daughter's part in it.

"Oh, Sophie, what the hell are you doing here?" She cast a wary eye at the large brick dwelling nestled behind a fence of tall pine trees. *Other than setting yourself up for more parental ridicule,* she added silently.

Perhaps a part of her was hoping that news of her pending promotion might soften the Hails' viewpoint toward her job. After all, she'd be more of a shot-caller than an order-taker, right?

The question strengthened her resolve and provided the necessary motivation for her to leave the car. As she began a search for her house keys on the silver ring she carried, she thought of Santigo.

How would he react when she told him of the promotion? she wondered. When? Sophia slowed her steps. Was she so certain they'd see each other again? Was it even wise to move ahead there? Sophia rolled her eyes, issuing a quiet order to herself to shut up. Wise or not, she missed the man's touch far too much to deny herself the possibility of enjoying it again.

Sophia gave a quick, decisive toss of her head and moved to unlock the front door. It opened before she could touch it, and Sophia smiled at the unexpected guest who stood on the other side.

Laureen Bradford was obviously caught up in her own thoughts if her jumping at the sound of Sophia's greeting was any clue.

"Oh!" Laureen gushed. "Sophia, honey, what a nice surprise."

Sophia bought Laureen Bradford's surprise; though there was more emotion mixed in than she could pinpoint. It was just as well since Veronica Hail was emerging at the door.

"Sophie, oh, baby, thank God."

The greeting was a far cry from the one Sophia had expected from her mother.

"Laur, what do you say we run this by Sophia?" Veronica smoothed a hand along the sleeve of the woman's burgundy floral-print blouse. "If there's a way, she'll know."

Laureen sniffled. Closing her eyes, she bowed her head, which sent a few tufts of her feathered hair into her round, milk-chocolate face. She nodded. "I'll get the papers from the car. Thank you, Sophie," she whispered while hurrying past.

"What happened?" Sophia asked her mother as she watched Laureen move down the long brick driveway.

"Her boy Kenny got himself arrested for stealing a car." Veronica sighed, smoothing five fingers along the tapered edges of her short hair, which accentuated a lovely oval face.

"Arrested?" Sophia cast a reflexive look across her shoulder. "Isn't he on his way to college?"

"Not if he's convicted over this."

Veronica Hail and Laureen Bradford had been friends for years. Laureen's small yet successful soul food restaurant was a yearly participant at the Reed House dinners. The women had launched a friendship while Laureen was preparing to showcase her cuisine during the first Reed House event.

"Oh, honey, I'm sorry." Veronica seemed to remember herself and pulled her daughter into a hug. "This is such a good surprise." She applied a few brisk rubs to Sophia's back. "It's chilly out here. Let's get inside."

I guess it can wait another day. Sophia decided against sharing her news. She acknowledged that she was being a wimp, but being on the receiving end of parental ridicule was never fun. She was preparing to follow her mother inside when her mobile vibrated. Tigo.

Sophia let the phone shake twice more so as not to appear too eager for the call. Who the hell was she kidding with this stuff?

"Hey, Tig." She congratulated herself on the coolly delivered greeting.

"I was wondering whether high-powered detectives ever took coffee breaks?"

Stop being a wimp, Sophie, she urged herself silently. "I'm, uh…actually no longer a high-powered detective."

The silence that followed was lengthy and meaningful.

"You didn't quit." His hushed tone was shrouded in disbelief.

Sophia couldn't tell whether he sounded more hopeful or stunned. "No. They…they actually offered me the chief of detectives post."

Laughter sounded without hesitation. "That's great!"

Sophia thought he actually sounded happy.

"To hell with a coffee break—this deserves a real celebration."

Sophia pressed the phone into the front of her blouse and moved aside to hold the door for Laureen Bradford, who was returning with folders in the crook of one arm.

"Miss Laur, would you tell Mama I'm on my way?" Sophia asked, smiling when the woman nodded. She put the phone back to her ear.

"I really don't want to make a big deal of it."

Santigo snorted out a laugh. "Precisely why you're not in charge of it. What time are you done at the station?"

"Well, I'm not sure—"

"Call me when you are. Go home, get dressed and I'll be over to get you maybe around seven?"

"Seven sounds good."

"Sounds good to me, too."

The connection was severed before Sophia could speak another word. No matter, she could hear her mother calling out to her.

"And neither of them had prior offenses?" Sophia inquired as she scanned one of the folders Laureen had brought in from her car. The women sat in Veronica Hail's sunroom; it had been made golden that day by the lamps required due to the overcast skies.

"No." Laureen Bradford sniffled against the tissue she'd been using to dab at her nose. "No, no, they're both good boys."

"Oswald Stowe." Sophia read the judge's signature on one of the papers.

Laureen nodded as she sniffled again. "The public defenders told us he was pretty easygoing and that everything should work out since the boys were first offenders. They said it should never have come to this."

"Making a statement for his public image maybe…." Sophia guessed. She didn't realize she'd spoken aloud until she heard Laureen Bradford gasp.

"Oh, Miss Laur, I'm sorry." Sophia eased an apologetic look toward her mother. Scooting to the edge of the rose-colored armchair she occupied, she reached over to pat the woman's knee. "I'll look into it and see what I can do," she promised.

Laureen blinked, and her teary eyes began to sparkle with hope. "Thank you, baby."

Sophia nodded again and then left her mother to console her friend.

"Baby girl!"

Sophia heard the familiar call within minutes of leaving the sunroom. Her father was on his way down the corridor toward her.

"How is it in there?" Gerald Hail asked, cocking his head toward the sunroom door.

Sophia cast a forlorn look toward the door, as well. "I don't know what I can do, but I'm gonna try to help."

Gerald nodded. "They'll appreciate it. Your mother's very worried."

"I'm sorry I bothered you guys today."

Squeezing his daughter's upper arms, Gerald stood back

on his long legs and regarded Sophia with a curious stare. "What's up?" he probed.

"Daddy—"

"What?"

Sophia shifted her weight. "It's probably not the best time to get into it now."

"Now you *have* to tell me." Gerald folded his arms over his broad chest, causing the jacket of his nylon warm-up suit to rustle. "You know I won't let up till you tell me."

Sophia bowed her head, inhaling her breath and courage. "They offered me the job as chief of detectives."

Gerald let out a "Whoop!" that had his daughter jumping. Moments later, he'd pulled Sophia into a crushing hug and swung her in a semicircle.

"Are you serious?" Sophia couldn't have hidden her disbelief had she tried.

"Are *you?*" Gerald countered, pushing back a mahogany curl that clung to Sophia's cheek. "Do you know how much that job of yours worries us? Now we can rest easier."

Sophia's smile was curious. "What are you saying, Dad?"

"Well, hell, as chief you can put your lil' butt behind a desk instead of out there in the street."

"Daddy..." Sophia grimaced at her father's declaration. "I'm still a cop, you know?"

"Sure you are." Gerald gave Sophia's chin a playful bump with his fist. "And now you're a cop who doesn't have to put her life on the line every day."

Sophia's phone picked that moment to vibrate. Gerald squeezed his daughter's wrist when he saw the mobile's faceplate glow.

"You get that and we'll talk later." Gerald kissed her forehead and then continued his trek down the long hall.

"Hail." Sophia answered before the call was sent to voice mail. She hadn't recognized the displayed number and was still rather dumbfounded when the man on the other end of the line began to speak.

"I'm sorry, Mr...?"

"Apologies, Detective." The man chuckled. "I'm sure you're running in so many crazy directions right now. Lem Chenowith here. I've just been hired as head of your style team. We'd like to schedule some time to meet and get acquainted. What works best with your schedule?"

"Uh..." Sophia was scratching the fine hair smattered along her temple. "Mr. uh—"

"Chenowith," Lem promptly supplied.

"Mr. Chenowith. Style team?"

"At your service. Now, what's a good time for us to drop by for a chat?" the man went on, with no thought that what he said was in any way out of the ordinary.

"Mr. Chenowith, I'm sorry but I think you have the wrong number. I—"

"Detective Hail, my team and I have been brought on board by the commissioner's office. We've been hired to keep our new chief of Ds looking her best."

Sophia stopped in the foyer and leaned against the wall. She pulled the phone away from her ear just briefly before continuing the strange conversation. "Mr. Chenowith—"

"Lem, please."

"I think there's been a mistake." Sophia exchanged scratching the hair at her temple for massaging the bridge of her nose. "The last thing I need is help getting dressed." She laughed at the absurdity of it all.

"Trust me, Detective, I certainly understand. Most people are very put off by the suggestion that their wardrobe isn't up to par."

Sophia bowed her head and gave it a shake.

"But don't you worry," Lem continued right along. "You just leave it all to me, and I promise you won't be disappointed."

"I'm sure I won't."

Lem found nothing to criticize in the flat way Sophia voiced the phrase and took her words to mean that all was well.

"We look forward to seeing you tomorrow, Chief."

"Sure thing." Sophia gave a mocking two-finger salute. At that point, she was so exasperated that she didn't care to argue any further. "Mr. Chen—Lem."

"Very good."

"Look, Lem, I'm in the middle of something—"

"Yes, yes, of course. We'll talk tomorrow."

Sophia could only stare at the phone once the connection ended. She felt as if she'd just been through a whirlwind. She was pushing off the wall to head for the front door when Veronica arrived in the foyer.

"Ma—" Sophia found herself pulled into a tight squeeze before she could say anymore.

"Congratulations! Your daddy just told me all about it." Veronica danced in place after she released her daughter from the embrace.

Sophia could tell from her mother's elated expression that she was happy for the same reasons as her father. After the dizzying conversation with the head of her new style team, Sophia was in no mood to make an issue of it.

"How's Miss Laur?" Sophia asked instead.

The glee Veronica showed began to dim. She tugged at the oversize cuffs on the white pin-striped blouse she wore and glanced across her shoulder. "All this hit her and Les out of nowhere. Ken's such a good boy. Sophia, honey, there has to be some kind of mistake." She clasped her hands and propped them against her chin. "Hopefully there's some way the boys can make up for it without going to jail."

Sophia didn't bother to tell her mother that the chances of that sort of break were bleak for two black kids.

"Don't worry, Mama. I'll look into it. We'll find a way."

Sophia nodded past the woman's shoulder. "You keep Miss Laureen calm. If she thinks of anything, she can call me."

"I will, honey, and you and I should make some time to discuss the celebration party."

Sophia ceased retrieving keys from her pocket. "Celebration for what?"

"Ha! Your promotion, of course."

"Ma. No."

"But, honey—"

"I don't want to bring a lot of attention to this."

"If anything deserves to be celebrated, it's this." Veronica posted her fists on her slender hips. "After years of putting your life on the line, you're being rewarded for it. Time to let someone else go into certain death for a change."

"Is that the time?" Sophia barely glanced at her wristwatch and turned for the door again.

"We need to discuss this, baby. I'm thinking of something intimate. Right here at the house."

"Mama, I'm in a hurry. I've got a lot to do before tonight."

"Oh?" The last piqued Veronica's rampant curiosity regarding the private lives of her daughters. "Anything exciting?"

Sophia shrugged, deciding to feed the woman's interest. "Dinner with Santigo Rodriguez."

Veronica's gasp filled the foyer, and glee illuminated her face once more. She was so overjoyed that she could only clasp her hands and press them to her chest.

Sophia took advantage of her mother's rare bout of speechlessness. "See you later." She kissed Veronica's cheek and hurried out the door.

"Now that *is* strange." Detective Sergeant Jofi Eames rubbed the stubble on his jaw and frowned. "Are you sure the guys haven't passed the man's bench before?"

"Nah." Tigo gave a slow shake of his head. "Not so much

as a parking ticket between the two of them. These are two of the good ones, Jof."

Tigo's meaning was clear, and the detective nodded his understanding. "Could be some kind of election or publicity stunt." Jofi reared back in his desk chair. "It could put him in a rough spot if he's seen as a softy on car thieves."

"Well, they'll cross that bridge soon enough. Families just want 'em granted bail. They're no flight risks, Jof, and…" Santigo's words trailed into silence when he saw Sophia arrive on the floor.

"I'll take this to mean the discussion's over?" Jofi smirked at his friend's captivated expression.

"Sure." Tigo left the metal chair he'd taken next to Jofi's desk. "You can take it from here."

Jofi grinned. "Why, thanks for your vote of confidence."

Focusing on Jofi, Tigo smirked and moved to shake hands and hug his old friend.

"I'll call if I make any headway," Jofi promised as Tigo headed out of the cramped, dank office space.

Tigo found Sophia leaning against her desk and browsing a file. His single knock sent her head lifting, eyes widening at the sight of him.

"Did I get our date wrong?" She quickly pushed to her feet.

Tigo raised his hands. "You're good—don't worry. I had other business and thought I'd drop by and congratulate you in person, Lieutenant."

"Well, are we still going out?" Sophia didn't care how anxious she sounded.

"Mmm-hmm…" The confirmation trailed off into quiet when he dipped his head to kiss her.

"My walls are glass," she reminded him, breathless and already curling her fingers around his jacket lapels to bring him closer.

He grinned, the gold flecks in his dark eyes sparkling with

devilish intent. "We should give 'em a good show then. Don't you think?" His tongue was enticing hers into a naughty battle before she had time to respond to his question.

Sophia managed a shaky moan as her tongue tentatively answered the call from his. Her heart thudded, heavy in her chest, the sound reverberating to her ears. Mere moments passed before she was kissing him with sheer lust and need fueling the gesture.

Tigo exercised the cooler head then and tugged on the hem of Sophia's short-waist blazer to draw her down. "I'll see you tonight," he promised, smiling into her lovely dark face while brushing his thumb across her well-kissed mouth. The playfulness returned to his gaze, and he shrugged as if skeptical.

"What?" Sophia knew she sounded dazed and dumbfounded. What the hell... He did that to her.

Tigo expelled an exaggerated sigh and focused on a curl that had found its way down inside her shirt. "We're on for tonight, unless the hard-core detective gets called away on assignment."

"Hmph." She rolled her eyes. "Haven't you heard? I'm now the hard-core *chief* of detectives." She blew an unruly curl from her forehead. "Getting called away on assignment and hurling myself into the lines of fire are now things of the past." She massaged the middle of her forehead. "At least they would be if my parents could have their way." Her mounting frustrations cooled to a simmer as if quelled by magic when her gray eyes settled once again on the enticing curve of his mouth. She bit her upper lip, hungry for the pleasure of another kiss.

Santigo was more interested in the Hails' reaction. "What'd they say?"

"Nothing bad." Sophia leaned against the desk. "I don't think they've ever been happier with me."

"Well, isn't that good?" Tigo sat next to her, nudging her

shoulder with his. "It's better than having them give you grief over it, right?"

"I don't know. Is that why *you* seem so thrilled?"

"It is."

Sophia's jaw dropped over the easy admission.

Tigo took her parted lips to mean she craved another kiss, which she did. He obliged, but only for a sweet moment. Then, he stood and brushed his nose across hers once, twice...

"Be ready by seven." His voice was a gruff whisper and then he was gone.

"Oh, boy..." Sophia groaned.

Chapter 4

"Hey, L.T."

Sophia turned and smiled curiously at the tall uniformed man heading toward her. He was excessively tall; he towered over her own five-eleven height.

"Officer," she greeted.

"Alvin Keele, ma'am," the young man shared once he'd moved closer. "Kelly Fields is my girlfriend."

Sophia nodded as she eyed the officer. "You seem to have a very good woman in your corner."

"Yeah…" Alvin grinned sheepishly and studied his shiny black shoes. "We met the day I graduated from the academy. Kelly's dad, Henry Fields, was one of my instructors."

"I see." Sophia nodded a bit more enthusiastically. "Well, she's a smart girl to go after the best in the bunch."

"She is," Alvin agreed, but something dimmed in his smile. "She stuck by me even when it looked like I was on my way to being part of the worst of the bunch."

"That sounds ominous." Sophia crossed her arms over her

chest. Her thoughts rested on Kelly, returning to the girl's manner the day they had spoken in the break room at the station.

"She, uh, made a point of thanking me one day when we talked." Sophia was relying on her cop's intuition, which told her there was more to the young woman's gratitude than met the eye. "Did that have something to do with you, by any chance?"

Again, Alvin cast his pale blue stare toward the floor and nodded. "Thank you for shutting it all down, ma'am." His voice was almost inaudible. "I could've been caught up in it so fast if you hadn't."

Sophia blinked sharply, inwardly acknowledging that her intuition was dead-on. "The money laundering. Someone approached you about it? Who?"

"It was Mike Cana, ma'am."

Sophia deflated a bit. Detective Mike Cana was already behind bars, where he'd hopefully remain for a long time given his part in the crime. She needed fresh intel and silently admitted that she was terribly anxious to close this down tight. The sooner she did, the sooner she could see what was in store for her with the new job and for her and Santigo.

"It's not over, is it?" Alvin watched Sophia as though his own intuition was at work.

"You've got good cop instincts already, Officer."

Alvin beamed over the compliment. "That's what Sergeant Fields said at the academy. Am I right, ma'am?"

Sophia cast a casual look over her shoulder. "There could be more rotten apples needing to be shaken out of the tree."

"My career could've been over before it started." Alvin's tone was firm, his expression set with a serious intensity. "All I'd have had to show for it would've been a jail cell."

Sophia patted his arm. "We're all glad it didn't come to that."

"Still doesn't sit right with me, L.T. Other cops could get

caught up in this, some before they even have a chance to learn *how* to be cops."

"You're right." Sophia's tone and demeanor were somber. "Alvin, please know that this means as much to me as it does to you. We've made a lot of headway. We'll shut the rest of it down. You can count on that."

"I want in, L.T."

"Alvin—"

"I know what I'm saying, and I want in." He stepped closer. "Whatever I can do fo help you get the rest of them."

That he was serious went without saying. She watched him through narrowed eyes. "Do you have a partner, Officer?"

"Elzbeta Croft."

"You trust her?"

"Yes. Yes, very much, ma'am."

Satisfied by the answers, Sophia looked over her shoulder again before she spoke. "Meet me tomorrow night at Mathers. You know it?" She asked.

Alvin nodded, recognizing the name of the bar and grill outside the city limits. The establishment was frequented by much of the city's factory workers.

Alvin almost broke into a smile, but he made a conscious effort not to appear too giddy. "Thanks, L.T." He moved to shake her hand briefly before he walked away.

For the second time that day, Sophia felt the rush of excited uncertainty claim her. "Oh, boy…" she breathed again.

Judge Reginald Creedy was a gregarious sort who loved to tell bawdy jokes almost as much as his old friend Santigo Rodriguez. The two met for a late lunch that afternoon and spent the first half of the date catching up and cracking gibes that had their waiter laughing as much as them as he saw to the needs of his customers.

Reginald Creedy was no slouch, though. The man had a reputation for running his courtroom in an effective, efficient manner. He also had a rep for fairness and professionalism. Lawyers who argued before him, be they for the prosecution or the defense, were forewarned to come prepared to Judge Reggie Creedy's court or pay a costly penalty.

Judge Creedy appeared more like what defendants and counsel were used to once Tigo had told his friend about the two young first-time offenders who were currently serving time in the county jail.

"Did they do it?" Reginald asked, grimacing when Tigo said it looked that way.

"What do the families want?" Reginald angled his wide frame back in the chair and tapped out a monotone melody on the tablecloth. "If those boys are found guilty, then I'm afraid they'll do some time."

Tigo was stroking his jaw as he concentrated on Reginald's outlook. "Does the crime justify them being held without bail?"

"It's often at the judge's discretion." Reginald raised his fine brown brows while considering the answer. "It does seem a bit excessive to not release the kids. They don't seem to have the means to disappear before trial, good kids before this, no priors…"

"The presiding judge could be trying to lay groundwork for election time, for friends seeking new terms."

"Yeah." Reginald clenched a fist. "A lot of my colleagues dust off their crusader's caps during times like these. What's the judge's name again?"

"Stowe. Oswald."

"Right. He's usually pretty easygoing. A bit too much so in my opinion." Reginald shrugged.

"The parents would be happy to have the boys out on bail. At least it'd be a start."

Reginald laid his fingers atop his belly and the rust-colored tie lying across it. "I'll see what I can do, San, but I can't make promises."

Tigo nodded. "Understood. I'm working on getting the new counsel. Right now they're being represented by public defenders. I'd appreciate whatever you can do."

The men were shaking hands across the table when their smiling waiter arrived with the hearty entrées they'd ordered.

Santigo's genuine smile broadened a smidge when Sophia opened her apartment door to him that evening.

"Did I need to specify 7:00 p.m. or a.m.?" He took in her scant attire of curve-hugging sleep shorts and a faded metallic-colored tee.

"I feel like staying in and hoped you'd feel the same." To make her point, she moved to link her arms around his neck.

Faintly, Tigo recalled what Linus had said about him and Sophia getting sex out of the way so they could *hear* one another without all the tension.

He couldn't say he was totally against the idea. He wasn't against the idea at all for that matter. She smelled so good and felt even better, he thought, in awe of how she could be so satiny soft and pliant in his arms and then switch gears in a heartbeat to a determined, hard-as-nails cop.

"Please say we can stay in," Sophia murmured against his ear, not giving one damn about how needy she may have sounded.

Her entire body screamed for him or...well, it would have been if that were possible. She breathed him in, losing herself in his essence and feeling that strip away all the anxieties and frustrations heaped on by her day.

"Please, Tig." She resorted to begging again.

Pliant indeed. Santigo felt his intentions shift as thoughts of going out for the night morphed into other preferences.

"Damn it," he growled, taking her neck in one hand to hold her steady for his kiss.

She tingled. Happiness, satisfaction, passion—all the good

things filled her, swirling like a summer breeze. The things she'd missed…

Sophia curved her fingers about the lapel of the silver-gray jacket he wore over a white shirt opened at the collar. Firmly, she tugged, bringing him into her place and pushing the door shut behind him.

Tigo groaned something incomprehensible and cupped her derriere, which filled the sleep shorts and his palms. He squeezed her into him. She fit against him perfectly. She always had. Losing another tether on his restraint, Santigo turned the tables and held her against the door.

Mingled gasps and moans colored the air. Tigo inhaled the missed scent of the spot below her ear, along her neck, the base of her throat… Sophia draped her leg over his hip, and he caught on, holding it there as he began to thrust against her.

"Can we stay in, please?" she repeated the request.

Tigo didn't want to answer or even think about an answer. He was thrusting his tongue in her mouth with such determination it was as though he were ravenous for her. Still, a frown claimed the spot between his sleek brows.

More than anything, he wanted to say yes, to grant her request and just take what she was offering and forget the rest. Impossibly, he deepened the kiss. Bringing both hands to her chest, he weighed the bouncy, braless mounds.

She was kissing him hungrier still, mindless and lost in the sensations his touch, his mere nearness, evoked. Still, she wasn't so far gone that she didn't work to remove the faded tee when he fondled her breasts.

"No…Sophie, stop." Tigo covered her hands on the hem of the tee. She'd already raised it enough so that the backs of his hands brushed the bare, satiny flesh of the mahogany-dark mounds. He cursed, hesitating over the next thrust of his tongue. Again, he asked her to wait.

Sophia was still deep in the throes of the kiss. She licked

and suckled at his tongue, nudging his nose with hers until his grip on her hands tightened. Finally, she tuned into his words.

"What's wrong?" She was understandably breathless.

"Sophia, please." He was the one begging and with good reason. She was still rubbing against him. He had no weapons against the expectant, desire-filled look in her exquisite eyes.

"Go get dressed," he said, bowing his head as weariness took over.

"You don't want to go," she voiced the soft, coaxing argument. She curved her fingers into the waistband of his trousers and began a provocative grind against the alluring bulge beneath his zipper.

Sophia added a lurid suckling to Tigo's earlobe, and all strength abandoned his legs. He braced his hands behind her on the door for support.

"Let's stay here." Her mouth was on his ear. Blindly, she searched for his arm, tugging at it, seeking his hand and squeezing when she found it, guiding it to the part of her body that wanted him most.

Locating strength from some unknown realm of his psyche, Tigo fisted the hand she'd taken captive. Muscles clenching along his strong jaw, he pulled back.

"Get dressed, Sophia." He issued the command and left her standing at the door.

Blinking out of her dream state, Sophia observed him with a different kind of intensity. At once, she recognized the rigid set of his shoulders. He wouldn't tell her a thing, and it would be hopeless to try and figure out what exactly was going on with him. She'd have no other choice but to wait.

She rested her palm on the door and pushed off it. "I'll be right back."

Tigo kept his back turned, listening to her hurried exit from the living room. He waited until he heard a door close somewhere in the back of the apartment and then allowed himself to breathe. Regaining a measure of calm, he went to the dual-sided chrome refrigerator in the kitchen and rooted around inside until he found a bottle of cranberry juice.

A quick scan of the cabinets turned up no alcohol to spike it with, so he took it as it was. Another door slammed in the distance, and Tigo's mouth curved into a smirk against the rim of the bottle. He felt no humor toward the situation, knowing she was just as pissed off at him as he was with himself. Rolling his eyes, he pressed the bottle to his forehead and sighed. "Tigo, what the hell are you doin'?"

"This is nice," Tigo complimented the frock Sophia had selected for their dinner outing. The formfitting number encased her svelte frame like an amber-colored glove. The chiffon under lace subtly deceived an onlooker into believing that he was seeing more than he should.

The gown did an exceptional job of enhancing Sophia's rich, dark coloring and the gloss of her curls. Tigo rubbed his fingers along the fringe of a sleeve that covered half her hand. His stare was fixed on the rise and fall of her chest.

Sophia retracted her hand and moved it to her lap beneath the elegantly set table for two. "Not according to my style team." She sighed.

Tigo knew that he had confused her and that he needed to be straight up about what he really wanted. Sex would be a fleeting delight if they indulged first and then he told her that he wanted more and she…denied him. Just then, though, he was more intrigued by her previous words.

"Style team?" Amusement crept into his beautifully set stare.

"Style team." Sophia observed the gracefully furnished dining room with its golden lighting and electric candelabras amid a mocha-and-cream color scheme. "They were hired to *ready me* for the public."

"I'm impressed." Tigo grinned while rearing back in the large, cushioned chair he occupied.

"At least one of us is. Maybe I'll feel the same once I'm over feeling insulted."

"Insulted?"

Sophia only waved her hand to indicate she wasn't in the mood to go into it.

"Will you tell me if I promise not to laugh?"

The persuasive lilt to his soothing deep tone dissolved Sophia's refusal.

"I'm starting to see why my parents are so happy about my new job." She wrinkled her small nose. "They think I'll be a figurehead." *So do you,* she silently tacked on in reference to Santigo.

"Why do you think they feel that way?"

"Lem—Lem Chenowith, head of my style team," she clarified. "He kept going on and on about press conferences, dinners, photo ops…" She rolled her hand lazily, then waved off the list in a huff. "I'm to put on a new face for the Philly P.D."

"And what a face…" Tigo commended.

His words instantly returned Sophia to her apartment and the memory of trying to take the man out of his clothes. In moments, she was softly reminding herself that she wasn't the wide-eyed college student head over heels for her cute boyfriend. She wasn't the green fresh-from-the-academy police officer, either. Life was a precious commodity in her business and so was time. She wasn't of a mind to waste it on daydreaming about passion, no matter how provocative it was.

"Why won't you sleep with me?" she asked.

Santigo's cool demeanor grew just a touch heated around the edge if the grinding at his jawline was any evidence. "They're things we should talk about first," he said.

His answer made her heart lurch. She had a fine idea of what those *things* were. At least half of them surely had to do with her job.

"I won't be a figurehead, Tigo."

The waitress arrived with their drinks, and the woman

made no secret of how much she was enjoying Santigo's presence. Not surprisingly, she basically ignored his date, setting down Sophia's drink with so little finesse that some of the liquid sloshed up over the sides of the glass.

Sophia made no issue of it and grabbed a napkin to dab at the spill.

"*This* took long enough," Tigo chastised. He was intentionally curt with the waitress when she stressed that he let her know if he needed *anything* else.

"Is your wine cold enough, Detective?" he asked while the waitress stood tense and embarrassed.

In spite of her agitation, Sophia could have kissed him. "It'll pass." She'd already dismissed the vampy server.

The woman made quick work of handing out their menus. Then she tugged at the hem of her black uniform dress and promised to return right away.

"Soon I'll be able to call you chief." Tigo kept his eyes on the leather-bound menu.

"It's more than a title." Sophia also kept her attention on the menu she held. "At least it'll be more than a title to *me*." She set down the menu and tapped her fingers against a glossy page.

"I remember how much I admired Paul Hertz, the way he did the job. He was chief of Ds and still got down in the mud with his men to make a bust." She grinned and took a swallow of the white wine. "I'm probably the only one who believed it had to do with stopping crimes. He probably wanted to be first on the scene to grab his share of the take."

Tigo had been watching her with concern shadowing his very attractive face. "Don't let this jade you, babe."

"It's not the job that's jading me, but you and my parents who think I'll just be sitting behind a desk and looking pretty all day."

Tigo nodded as if conceding her point. He leaned forward to rest his forehead against the tips of his fingers. "You know you'd be pretty whether or not you were sitting behind a desk."

"Well, now that depends on how active I'd be, doesn't it?" She issued the challenge softly. "I plan to remain highly active, Tig, so if that's one of the *things* we need to talk about, I'm sorry." She smoothed her hands across suddenly chilled arms. "Nothing's changed. I'm still a cop. It's all I want to be."

"All?" His fingers left his brow to flare out into a questioning wave. "Are you saying there's no room for anything or anyone else?"

"Not if they expect me to choose." She kept her eyes on her glass.

"What if they don't expect you to choose?"

"Detective Hail!"

Sophia was caught between surprise at the sound of her name being bellowed and shock over Santigo's question. With no small effort she looked away from him and over to the stocky Caucasian man heading toward the table.

"Lieutenant Arnold." She stood to take the man's outstretched hands.

"I hear congrats are in order." The older man grinned while shaking both of Sophia's hands.

"Nothing's been set in stone yet, Lou."

"Always so modest," Glenn Arnold's slightly bloodshot blue-gray eyes twinkled with knowing. "You should be proud, kid."

Sophia clasped her hands at her waist when they were released from Glenn Arnold's mildly damp ones. "It doesn't sit too well with me that I'm bypassing more experienced candidates." She waved her hand with a flourish. "You're among that group."

"Aggh." Arnold rolled his eyes. "Never had any aspirations for the glamorous life. I think the powers that be chose wisely."

"I appreciate you saying that, sir, but I think you'd be among the minority. I'm sure a lot of folks are unhappy about this, especially since most of them think I'm a traitor because of what happened with Paul."

"Idiot." Arnold grimaced. "Hertz was stupid and careless. Got too full of himself trying to play in the big leagues. He should've been watching his back. You have nothing to feel guilty or uneasy over, Detective. I believe you'll be a good fit, and you have my support."

Sophia smiled and took the man's hands when he extended them again. "Thank you, sir."

Glenn Arnold nodded toward Santigo before he moved on.

"What?" Sophia questioned Tigo's unreadable look when she'd reclaimed her place at their table.

"Someone's givin' you a hard time over that mess with Cole?" he asked.

"Some nasty looks." She shrugged. "Nothing more than that. What?" she queried in a teasing manner. "You volunteering to be my bodyguard?"

The waitress returned then, her persona far less vampy than it had been earlier. Tigo handled the orders before Sophia could even open her menu.

"Let's dance." He offered her his hand once the server had gone.

Sophia accepted, placing her hand in his when he rounded the table. Tigo pulled her arm through the crook of his and kept her close to his side on the way to the dance floor. Along the way, they saw several people who either knew Sophia, Tigo or both of them. Sophia was thankful that no one remarked on whether or not they were an item again.

Such questions would have been unnecessary anyway. All anyone had to do was take note of the way they came together on the dance floor. Sophia nestled against Tigo's lean, athletic frame as they swayed to the sultry rhythms from the all brass house band. Regardless of the delicious emotions surging through her from their closeness, Sophia could feel the tension radiating from Tigo's shoulders.

"With all the people you know, I should have *you* looking into the Cole thing," she mused to break the tension.

"What Cole thing?" Santigo's expression merely darkened.

"The D.A.'s office is concerned about the deal he wants to make. Paula doesn't want me on the investigation, not officially. So I'm getting help."

"Thank you, Paula."

Sophia smiled at his grim celebration. "You're still honest. Guess we'll always have that." She bit down on her lip. Being so close, she was unable to resist a moment to indulge in what they'd enjoyed before leaving her place. Her fingers toyed around inside the open collar of his shirt, fingertips grazing the chain around his neck.

"We had a helluva lot more than honesty, Soap."

Their dance took a more sensual turn then. Soon they were caught in the whirlwind of another kiss. Lips met in a tentative exploration, sweetly at first and then with greater urgency.

The restaurant was a dim, seductive place, especially where the dance floor was concerned. Tigo wanted to take full advantage of the simmering ambience and the beauty in his arms, but he clenched his hands at Sophia's waist to prevent them from cupping her bottom and squeezing to his content. Her soft moans as she tangled her tongue with his were growing impossible to walk away from.

"Sophie—"

"I know." She spoke the words in his mouth and then eased back with a sigh. "We need to talk first."

He smiled, tilting up her chin to inspect the lipstick that was surprisingly unsmudged. "Actually we need to eat first."

Sophia followed the path of his stare beyond her shoulder and saw that their food had arrived. Arm in arm, they left the floor.

Chapter 5

Sophia and Tigo were halfway through dinner when she accepted that he was in no mood for light conversation. She allowed it to last for the duration of the meal but had had enough of it by the time they'd returned to her apartment building.

"So is the silent treatment part of you being upset that the Cole case isn't completely closed?"

"I'm upset over the fact that you're goin' through a hard time because of it," he told her as the elevator doors opened on her floor.

"It's to be expected," she said airily as they took the corridor to her door.

"Since when have you gotten so used to being threatened?"

"Goes with the job." Sophia winced the second the words left her tongue. Clearly the response didn't sit well with her date. She could hear low growling sounds curling deep in his throat.

"You know, it's really not necessary for you to bring me to the door."

"Goes with the date," he threw back.

Sophia pressed her lips together until she'd unlocked the door and stepped inside. In the living room, she faced him with her arms spread.

"Safe and sound, so…"

Tigo ignored her hint and moved inside to look around.

"Everyone in the building knows I'm a cop, Tig," she called to his back as he moved deeper into the apartment. "Anyone else will know they've made a mistake walking up in here uninvited once I greet them with my gun." She grinned at the words, but she had sobered by the time he'd completed the inspection.

"Are you ready to be straight with me? Even a little?" Her weary tone matched the look in her eyes. "What do you want from me? Clearly not sex." Her lazy grin returned. "I've been throwing all this at you, and you haven't taken the bait yet."

Santigo's bottomless stare followed the graceful, somewhat playful sweep Sophia made with her hands along the length of her body.

She cleared her throat when she saw that her tease hadn't produced the desired response. "Damn it, Tig." She slapped her hands on her sides. "Even us seasoned detectives are no good at reading minds."

She'd scarcely gotten the words past her lips when he bolted across the room. Decision sharpened the intriguing mix of his features. Sophia tilted her head seconds before realizing his intent. Of course by then he'd already taken her wrist and jerked her in once, close.

"Tig—" It was all she had time to say before her mouth was occupied by his kiss. Instantly, she melted, and her body sang over his touch. But she was sick of being teased and drew on all of her willpower to break the kiss.

"Will you stay?" she asked once she'd pushed as far away as he'd let her.

His half-lidded gaze studied her upturned face, and then he leaned down to ply the soft flesh of her earlobe with gentle nibbles from his lips and perfect teeth. Against her ear, he spoke the words she'd waited to hear since the day she'd found him waiting in her office after eight years of distance.

"I'll do more than that," he promised her.

Then, the side zipper along her snug dress was handled with an expert, efficient touch. Once the bodice had parted from the back, Tigo dipped his head to graze his mouth along the line of her neck. He palmed one breast, his thumb assaulting the nipple that strained beneath a lacy bra cup.

Sophia kept one arm draped across his shoulder, her fingers toying in the cottony-soft dark waves that tapered at his neck. Her other hand was limp, hanging at her side. Tigo used her stance to his advantage, sliding the sleeve from her arm before unhooking the bra's fastening.

Sophia instigated a kiss and carried it out with shameless hunger. Standing on her toes, she sought to enjoy every nuance of the kiss, tilting her head this way and that while soft moans accompanied every languid thrust of her tongue.

Santigo cupped her arm and left the other to dangle at her side as he removed what remained of her dress. He held her away once the garment pooled about the champagne-colored platform heels she wore.

Sophia pressed her lips together and watched him take a slow perusal of her body. He kept both hands folded over her arms, and his dark head bowed in his study of her.

Sophia's gray stare was contemplative as she watched him with the same astuteness. Coolly she observed the slow rise and fall of broad shoulders beneath his jacket. She could tell that his breathing was growing ragged. The knowledge of that lent a triumphant lift to the corner of her bow-shaped mouth. When Santigo suddenly straightened to his full height and took her high against him, her heart surged to the back of her throat.

Eagerly, she swayed closer to ply him with a kiss, but he resisted. Instead, he kept his probing eyes on hers while carrying her toward the back of the apartment.

Sophia was so absorbed in the potency of his gaze that she hardly noticed him tumbling her into the four-poster queen bed. It took another few moments before she even realized that the bed had been turned down. She surmised that he must have taken care of that little chore during his earlier security check of the apartment.

"Turndown service." Her voice held a breathy quality laced with a hint of amusement. "That part of the date, too?"

His trademark easy grin returned. "It's the best part."

"That's right." She let her lashes flutter down as though she'd suddenly remembered. "I almost forgot."

"So did I."

Sophia heard the growling sound in his throat again and focused on his sinfully crafted mouth as it neared to entice hers into another kiss. She could have easily sizzled to his touch; she was so on fire for him.

She rarely indulged in wearing devilish undergarments. What for? The bulk of her days were spent in sensible pants and shirts, which were better suited for the rigors of her job. That night, she'd ventured into her rarely open sexy lingerie drawer and decided that the evening called for sheer stockings and matching garters.

Her panties and bra were the same material of her gown—lacy and see-through.

Sophia couldn't help but shiver at the decadent effects of being held by a fully clothed Santigo Rodriguez. For a woman whose life demanded strength and seriousness, indulging in a bit of stereotypical femininity was too sweet a respite to ignore.

Tigo took full advantage of Sophia's present attire. He

planned to have her screaming his name soon enough. For the moment, he wanted to hear her screaming for him to take her out of the sheer garments that were driving him out of his mind.

She was like a treat for him and him alone. Sharing was not an option—only enjoying. He wanted to enjoy every bit of her until he'd slaked his thirst, some of it anyway.

Sophia could hear her heart, the beats threatened to ravage her eardrums. The look Tigo fixed her with was *that* hungry, *that* passionate, *that* intentional. He never broke eye contact; even as he toyed with her garter fastening and the lacy tops of her stockings. He smirked when he saw her lips part in response to his fingers, which then skirted the edge of her panties.

Sophia pressed her head back into the pillow, moaning as he worked his thumb into the crotch of her panties. He nurtured himself by spending a few moments at her breasts while driving his thumb in slow, torturous rotations at her clit. A frenzy of sensation stirred at the dual caress. Sophia circled her hips on the tangled covers and played lazily in her hair as tiny moans rippled from her mouth.

"Tell me." He lifted his head to coax her. He wanted more than moans out of her. He could feel faint dampness against his thumb through the material of her panties.

"Tig…"

"There we go…" He sighed, smiling down at her in the most adoring manner.

"How's this?" He incorporated subtle pinches to the fleshy mound inside her underwear and bent his head to trail his nose along the curve of her jaw.

"Please, Tig…"

"What do you want from me?" He stretched his long, lean frame against hers. "To stop?" He ceased the maddening pinches of her clit and returned to the slow rubs.

"Mmm, no, no…"

He grinned and subjected her to intermittent rounds of pinching and stroking one of her most sensitive possessions. He braced himself on his elbow as he lay beside her, then brought his fingers to his brow. A look of utter fascination claimed his extraordinary features. She held him, entranced as he studied the effects his touch had on her expression.

"Tigo...mmm...please..."

His eyes narrowed, an amused and teasing element causing the dark orbs to sparkle. "Why won't you tell me what you're pleading for?" He hooked his middle finger into a side seam along her panties and slid downward to the middle of the garment.

Sophia bit her lip, curving her fists against his chest as her hips undulated clockwise and counter. When his finger finally made contact with her skin, she arched like a sensual bow.

"Ahh...so that's what you wanted...."

She was breathless and not ashamed to be on the verge of panting. Greedily, she clutched the wrist belonging to the hand that was at that point halfway inside her panties. Deftly, she attempted to instruct him, to encourage him to give her what she truly desired from his fingers.

"What's this?" Again, Tigo feigned confusion. "You pulling me away?" He pretended to withdraw.

"Stop..."

"If you insist." He pulled away even more.

She was on the verge of sobbing; need had turned her into an aroused wreck. Santigo finally took pity, and Sophia shrieked when he plunged his middle finger into the creamy well of sensation that he'd awakened at the crest of her thighs.

Her hands had weakened on his wrist and then slid away, depleted of any strength. She let them rest on the covers, only her hips maintained a sense of strength. They still arched and rotated in time to the exploration of his fingers—there were two inside her then.

Tigo knew his restraint was fast approaching its depletion point, as well. Still, he was captivated by the way she appeared as he played with her. God, he'd missed her! She had no idea how obsessed he was by the thought of a future with her. Never again would he be fool enough to risk losing that.

Sophia was steadily heading toward what had the makings of an incredible climax. She was so preoccupied by what his fingers were doing; there were three inside her. She was only somewhat aware of the fact that her underthings were slowly peeling away. She felt the hose rolling down her legs and heard the dull thud of pumps dropping to the floor.

Her eyes opened with a flutter of lashes when his fingers withdrew. She had no chance to blast him for it; they were instantly replaced by his tongue. The organ thrust hot and moist. Sophia curled her fingers into the top of his head to luxuriate in the pitch waves of satin covering his head.

His hands on her hips stifled any moves, and Sophia thought she'd go mad from the need to meet the heavy strokes his tongue made inside her body. Wild with frustration, arousal, desire, she began to play with her nipples and moaned at the feel of the tips still moist from his earlier attention.

Tigo was having none of that and slapped at her hands when he saw where they were. "Those are mine," he growled as he lowered his head again. The sound of his words vibrated from between her legs.

"Tig." Sophia grazed her nails through his hair and then bit her lip before sobbing his name again.

Once more, she found herself at the threshold of an awesome climax, and once more he denied her the pleasure. Tigo pushed himself up and set a knee between her thighs to prevent any thoughts she may've had to close her legs. He doffed the finely made silver-gray sport coat and shirt. He slapped at her hands when they ventured toward her sex, her nipples or any place that he felt was his and his alone to enjoy.

"Stay where you are." The order was soft, and he put his index finger beneath her chin, tipping back her head until her eyes met his. "Stay." He nodded, not leaving the bed until she'd reciprocated the nod.

He removed the rest of his clothes, tossing them aside once he'd produced several condom packets from his trousers. Returning to the bed, he sprinkled them down over Sophia's trembling mahogany-brown frame.

She watched him with a mix of longing, lust and love flooding her. The bed dipped in response to his weight when he settled back down next to her. She raked her nails across the array of striking abdominal muscles that flexed when he shifted closer and bit her lip at the sensation of skin on skin when he reclaimed his place between her thighs. Linking her arms around his waist, she stroked along his spine. Tigo stroked his own tune on Sophia's body, beginning at the column of her elegant neck, then at her collarbone and on to the swells of her bosom.

"Tig…" She arched her back when he cupped a breast. He squeezed while lightly circling his nose around the tip.

Sophia wriggled beneath the caress, hungry for him to take her nipple into his mouth. "Tigo." She nudged his lips with her nipple and loosed a breathless laugh when he obliged her unspoken plea.

Tigo groaned amid a round of mad suckling as she rocked her hips against his in a sensuous grind. He held both her breasts captive in his wide grasp. Focused, he tended them, teeth and tongue subjecting one bud to a lurid assault before abandoning it, leaving it glistening and pouting when he moved on to its twin.

Sophia glided her hand down between their bodies until she held the delicious thickness of his erection in her palm. She couldn't close her hand completely over him but satisfied herself by stroking the rigid-steel-under-satin organ that pulsated just slightly to her touch.

"Hell, Sophia." His perfectly shaped mouth slackened over her breast.

"You want me to stop?" It was her turn to tease.

That was a yes-or-no question, and neither answer was one Tigo was willing to give. Blindly, he smoothed a hand over the covers, searching for one of the condoms he'd tossed out earlier. It was all he could do to press the foil casing into Sophia's palm once he'd found one. His hand shook erratically, and that merely endeared him to the woman he held.

Sophia was no less affected, but she did manage to set their protection and guide him to the place they both sought.

Tigo captured Sophia's hips the moment he thrust, deep and branding inside her. Sensually slow, he cradled her bottom before circling his hands around her thighs and spreading them wider.

Sophia pressed her head even deeper into the pillows. His hold on her thighs deepened the penetration, and her moans were throaty, bold—she held back nothing. She wanted this man to know just how much he pleasured her.

Tigo had been simultaneously inhaling Sophia's scent and groaning his satisfaction from the crook of her shoulder. He raised his head to cup the side of her face. After studying her briefly, he dipped his head and brought his mouth down on hers, crushing her lips beneath a ravenous onslaught. Sophia worked happily to match the intensity of the kiss. Their lusty tongue-play matched the fiery tussle of their bodies—hips, legs and arms danced in a seductive presentation across the wrinkled covers.

Sophia's gasp hinged on a cry when she was suddenly turned on her stomach. Tigo closed his hand around a mound of her shoulder-length curls and took her from behind. Again, his handsome face was hidden in the crook of her neck. There, he nibbled at the tendrils of hair matted in the spot while his fingers snaked around her hip to seek out the bare patch of flesh at the juncture of her thighs.

Sophia's moans were muffled well into the pillows as Tigo took his time dishing out the dual caress. Somehow she managed to regain a measure of her control and slammed back into him, working hard and fast against him as she brought them to climax. Tigo cursed her wickedly as he succumbed to the effects of their united bodies. His hand flexed almost painfully on her hip as he came powerfully inside her.

The sounds of their mingled breaths were loud and ragged. Soon, exhaustion claimed them, and they drifted contentedly into the deep well of sleep.

Sophia merged from her dream state into waking and smiled. Usually, her day began when she jerked herself out of a restless slumber. Relaxation was unfortunately not a normal part of her bedtime hours. She moved to sit up and found that she couldn't. It was then that she discovered Tigo stifling her movement. He rested on her at an angle with his chest on her abdomen.

The tangled sheets were twisted deliciously around his lower half. Sophia smiled, feeling that slow course of relaxation welling up inside her again. She delighted in the gentle flex of the ropy muscles in his back and stroked him there softly so he wouldn't wake. His face was half-hidden beneath a pillow as he rested. His slow breathing was deep and hinted at a snore.

Sophia's light strokes beneath his shoulder blade must have stirred his ticklish senses, for he flinched a tad. A smile emerged, adding more definition to the gorgeous curve of his mouth.

"Payback's no fun," he slurred and shifted a small distance away from her touch.

"What?" Sophia pretended confusion while chasing him with her fingers. She shrieked when he pounced a few moments later and started a playful gnawing at her neck.

"Hmm." She gestured amid her giggles. "This doesn't feel like payback."

He switched gears, nibbling her ear while fondling the puckering flesh of her sex.

Sophia gasped. "That doesn't feel like payback, either."

"Sorry to hear that." His voice was a growl next to her ear. "Because I definitely need to find a way to thank you for last night."

"No thanks are necessary." She stretched like a lazy feline beneath him. "But I'll take it."

Santigo's caresses became more explicit, more exploratory. He suckled her earlobe, intermittently biting down into the softness with his perfect teeth. His middle finger swept across her folds slick with the moisture of her need; his thumb was making circular moves across her clit and causing her to squirm uncontrollably.

The sound of dull grinding began to work its way in among their soft whispers and drowsy laughter as another heated interlude took shape between them. Tigo ignored the sound easily; his thoughts and attention were wholly focused on Sophia's mahogany-toned breasts presently sheltering his darkly gorgeous face.

"Tig?" She frowned amid her ecstasy. "Is that you?"

"It is," he growled the suggestive confirmation into her breasts.

Sophia knew he was referring to the lengthy solidness of his flawless caramel-toned sex that nudged hers insistently.

"Sounds like a phone." Her voice was lazy, and she was happy to forget the phone and everything else when his growling tone touched her ears and she heard him tell her it could wait.

Tigo abandoned her breasts and kissed his way down the length of Sophia's body. Whisper-soft pecks streamed downward until he paused to repay her for the earlier tickling incident. His nose invaded her belly button just slightly, and he chuckled when she squirmed again.

Soon he was settling before the intimate treasure he sought. Gently, he stroked the satiny petals there. His index fingers spread the folds as though he were unwrapping a priceless package. As he'd done with her navel, he used the end of his nose to probe her core. He ignored the way she shuddered intensely beneath him during the provocative exploration. Sophia tried to tamp down the desire to orgasm; she wanted the treat to last...forever.

Tigo seemed insatiable as he plundered her. His tongue rotated, thrust and lapped obsessively. He could smell himself all over her, and the effect was powerful enough to drive him mad.

"Tigo I—I'm..." She tried to warn him of impending climax, but her verbal skills had deserted her.

Santigo didn't seem to care. He was intent on her coming apart in his arms. He continued to explore her, implanting heated strokes deep and possessively even as she bucked in the throes of an intense release.

When she'd come down from her high, the dull grinding of the phone was filling the air again.

"Guess I better get that," he groaned into her stomach.

Sophia pushed herself up while pushing Tigo to his back. "It can wait." She proceeded to rain kisses down his torso en route to repaying his splendid treat.

Chapter 6

Despite all her encouraging and creative designs to entice Tigo into spending the day in bed, Sophia couldn't convince him to give in. Furthermore, he surprised her by making note of the fact that she was a sought-after woman and that there were lots of people waiting on a meeting with the new chief of Ds.

The fact that such a thing had occurred to him, even enough to joke about, gave Sophia pause. If his new tolerant side was all an act, there would have been no need for him to perpetrate it beyond last night, right? Could he be for real? she wondered. Sophia didn't think she was ready to know his motives, not when she was having such fun becoming reacquainted with other things.

She stretched among the covers and only then did she think to check her mobile. She was stunned that she hadn't been called in to the station during the course of her exquisite night...and morning. Stretching once more, she admitted to herself that sometimes the fates were kind.

The doorbell rang just as the phone chimed, and she sucked her teeth. "So much for that." She pushed off the covers and reached for the slim phone. A frown tugged at the delicate arch of her brows when she saw the unidentified number.

"Yes?" she said after a few additional moments of debate. Male laughter filled her ear milliseconds later.

"Time to rise and shine, beautiful." Lem Chenowith's lively tone followed the laughter.

"I'll have to call you back, Lem." Sophia activated the phone's speaker and then jerked into the short black terry robe she'd pulled from her bedroom doorknob.

"Well, you could at least answer your door," he requested.

Again Sophia frowned. "How—" She closed her eyes. "Oh, no." Clicking off the phone, she padded barefoot through the apartment toward the front door.

Lem waited in the hall along with three people Sophia didn't recognize.

"Beautiful even in the mornings. Just like I thought." The man whirled past the door like a storm, and then he turned with a flourish and smiled. "Lem Chenowith at your service, Detective. And this is the rest of your team. Kendra Williams, Freddy Donald and, last but not least, Mr. Connor Denton."

Gracious to a fault, Sophia clasped her hands and nodded. "It's good to meet you all." She gave Lem a wilting smile. "This may not be the best time."

Lem rested a hand along the side of a baby-smooth jaw. "Well, we thought we'd wait until Mr. Rodriguez left before we disturbed you."

Her jaw dropped. "How did you…?"

Lem made a tsking sound. "You're in the public eye now, sweetheart. A local celebrity, if you will."

"That doesn't mean my sex life's an open book," she snapped, pleased at the firmness accompanying the words.

"We understand your frustration, Detective." Kendra Williams's smiling face was framed by a halo of short chestnut curls that bobbed when she nodded. "It's just that…a lot of people saw you both out for dinner together last night. And, if you don't mind my saying, when women think of Santigo Rodriguez, they think of a delicious fantasy. It'd be hard for anyone, any woman, to believe you guys just let it end at a good-night kiss."

Sophia shifted her weight as memories of those good-night kisses filtered her thoughts. Defeated, she slapped her hands to her sides. "Can I at least shower before we have our meeting?"

"We'll do you one better." Lem's brown eyes sparkled as he came over to drop an arm across her shoulders. "You take your shower while we set up out here."

"Set up?" Sophia stopped in her tracks.

"Now, now, don't worry." Lem urged her on toward the hall. "Have a luxurious shower and by the time you're done, we'll be ready to get started out here."

Realizing further clarification would not be forthcoming, Sophia conceded. Leaving the four strangers out front, she returned to her bedroom. There, she made quick work of stripping off the peach-colored sheets and tugging the matching comforter back in place across the bed. She shoved the linens into a hamper and then took a dainty .36 caliber from a hidden drawer in the closet. The firearm would be a nice companion until she got to know her "style team" a little better.

"I can't believe you found something so fast," Tigo told Judge Reginald Creedy as they shook hands later that morning in the judge's chambers.

Reginald shrugged. "We judges enjoy an intimate society."

"How intimate?" Tigo grinned.

"You really want to know?"

Tigo raised his hands defensively. "Save it. I should've known the robes served a purpose."

Reginald perched his large frame on the edge of his desk once a healthy round of laughter had quelled. "It's unfortunate that a judge's blemishes are usually better-known than his triumphs."

"That's the case with a lot of things." Tigo leaned back in the chair he'd selected and eyed the man warily. "How bad is it?"

"Bad enough to smell."

Tigo muttered a curse. "What'd you find?" he asked, rubbing his index and middle finger along the side of his nose.

With a sigh, Reginald reached back to grab a folder from his desk. "Turns out, my friend Ozzie is quite the Good Samaritan." He leafed through the folder. "He's been heartwarmingly fair to lots of defendants. Everyone knows this about him. He believes in redemption and offers second sometimes third chances."

"A felon's best friend," Tigo mused.

"Hmph. Good call. And that's what it'd appear to be... on the outside."

Tigo lifted his head a fraction. "More than a Good Samaritan?"

"Depends."

"On?"

Reginald tossed the folder back to the desk. "On whether there's a reason why he's been so kind to just under half the defendants in his courtroom over the past twenty months— all who work for Greenway Construction. All but one."

"Kenny Bradford," Tigo guessed. "So why didn't he qualify for the Stowe discount?" he asked after a measured silence. "Maybe because he didn't get pinched alone?"

"Ian Roche," Reginald noted. "But why? What's a judge have in common with a construction company?"

Tigo rested his elbows on his knees. "Whatever it is, it may be the reason why those kids are still sitting up in a jail cell."

* * *

Sophia finished her shower feeling uncommonly relaxed, refreshed and ready to start a new day. Until she remembered the four members of her style team waiting with their words of wisdom regarding all her fashion mistakes as of late.

In the bathroom, she toweled off quickly, moisturized and wrapped herself back in the terry robe. She opened the door, prepared to meet her fate, when it occurred to her that she might prove to be too much of a problem child for the new fashion quartet. They might even be kind enough to inform the commissioner's office that she was a lost cause.

She felt a bit more hopeful, and there was an added bounce to her step when she left the bathroom.

Her gray eyes widened when they landed on the ensemble hanging on the full-length mirror near her bed. She couldn't recall having the outfit in her closet, and she wondered if it was new. Closer inspection proved that the coordinating blazer, pants and wide-cuffed cream shirt had come right from her modest wardrobe.

"I think she likes it."

Sophia heard Kendra's voice and turned to find her and Lem huddled in the doorway.

"Bet you forgot you had those things," Lem said.

"I don't really take the time to think about what I'll wear the next day." She looked back at the outfit.

"Well, you won't have to think about it anymore as long as you've got us in your corner. Ah-ah-ah, stay in your robe. Freddy's got your breakfast ready, and after that Connor will do your hair and makeup."

"Is Freddy my cook?"

"Nutritionist," Kendra said. "We're leaving no stone unturned as far as your well-being's concerned."

"This is all so unnecessary," Sophia grumbled, blowing at a curl that had fallen free of her messy ponytail.

"You're important to a lot of people," Lem reasoned.

"I just don't think the taxpayers are gonna approve of a pricey figurehead."

Lem gave a nod to Kendra, then went to Sophia. With a reassuring squeeze to her wrist, he guided her into the living room and motioned for her to take a seat.

"Detective, before I accepted this job, I had a conversation with your superiors. I told them pretty much what you just said back there."

At Sophia's stunned look, Lem smiled and joined her on the sofa. "What they told me made me believe in the role I have to play here."

Sophia steeled herself. "And what is that?"

"It's important for people to feel secure." Lem studied his perfectly manicured nails, flexing them as he spoke. "In *this* day and time, it's especially important. It's curtains if people lose faith in their local government." He fixed her with an unwavering look. "You're to be the first step in strengthening that faith."

"And I need to look the part, right?"

"Detective, may I speak frankly?"

Sophia raised her hands and let them fall heavily into her lap. "Please."

Lem smoothed a hand across his shaved head. "Sophia, much of your newfound stature has to do with your work in Waymon Cole's arrest, but even more of it has to do with your looks. Many feel that putting a smart, beautiful cop on the face of this scandal, a scandal *you* helped to uncover, could be a huge win for city hall and for the city on the national scene." He shrugged. "My staff and I are here to help bring that to fruition."

"So all I have to do is look pretty?"

Lem tweaked her chin. "Look pretty and stay smart," he said just as Freddy walked into the living room with a tray loaded with fruits, cheeses, a large croissant and an even larger glass of orange juice.

"Let me guess." Sophia raised a finger. "All this was in my fridge and I just didn't know it?" She couldn't help but join in when the team laughed.

When Sophia arrived at Police Commissioner Ethan Meeks's office later that morning, she was surprised to find Paula Starker there along with Captain Roy Poltice and Chief of Police Dean Franklin. She jumped at the chance to pull Paula aside while the commissioner finished a call.

"What are you doing here?" Sophia hissed through clenched teeth.

Paula dismissed the question, as she was more interested in judging Sophia's attire. "Very nice, So-So. This'll look good on camera."

"What camera?" Sophia swung her head around but spied nothing out of the ordinary inside Meeks's elegant maple-paneled office.

"Calm down, girl. Everything's fine."

"Don't worry." Sophia gave Paula a sour look. "The figurehead is ready to play her role."

"Come again?"

"Forget it, Pauly. You took me off the Cole case to free me up for *this* nonsense, didn't you?"

Paula took Sophia by the arm and pulled her aside none too gently. "I took you off because there *is* something more to all that you dug up, but there are too many eyes on you now. We need to play this cool if we're gonna have a hope in hell of uncovering the rest of it." She gave a toss of her bobbed locks and straightened her stance. "If whoever else is involved in this wants to watch you so damn bad, you'll damn well give 'em a good *show*. Keep your enemies focused on all the flash and dazzle and they'll never see what you've got comin' up behind them."

Sophia glanced across her shoulder and saw that the commissioner was finishing up his call.

"Keep your mouth shut about this."

Sophia frowned back at Paula. "What are you trying to say?"

"You're playin' with the big boys now, and no one in this league should be trusted."

"You including yourself?"

Paula merely winked and sent a dazzling smile toward the three men across the room.

Chief of Police Dean Franklin rubbed his hands together and looked at Sophia. "I hope you have some good news for us, Detective?"

"Join us here at WPXI News 4 Philly live tomorrow at noon for full coverage of the press conference. Once again, stunning news direct from Commissioner Ethan Meeks's office. Detective Sophia Hail has just been named as Philly's new chief of detectives.... Back to you in the studio, Joseph."

Sophia groaned at the sound of her doorbell and prayed her building's usually top-notch security hadn't fallen down on the job and allowed one of the persistent reporters up to her floor.

The intimate meeting with Paula Starker and the gang at Commissioner Meeks's office had quickly turned into the "show" Paula had alluded to.

Sophia accepted the job, after which followed a quick round of handshakes and congrats. Commissioner Meeks made a call and, within minutes, the office filled with reporters from several local papers. The moment had passed in a relative blur. Sophia only recalled the rapid succession of camera flashes as she stood wearing a pasted-on smile. Meanwhile, the commissioner made the announcement and promised a more detailed discussion of the circumstances following her appointment during the next day's press conference.

She could barely recall the drive home. She hadn't expected to be blindsided quite so…blindly. She was also rather pissed at Paula for not better preparing her for the media blitz. She hadn't even gone into the precinct that day; she could only imagine the circuslike environment the place must have been in. More circuslike than it usually was anyway.

She'd been closed up in her apartment for over five hours. This was something she hadn't done in a long while. She'd even hidden her mobile deep in a sock drawer, not wanting to know who was calling or why. The landline was unplugged. She only connected to the outside world via television.

Now I know the need for the sudden makeover this morning. She pouted while making her way to the front door from the kitchen table, where she'd been watching the living room TV.

Sophia offered up a quick prayer for it not to be Lem or anyone else from her style team. Her heart soared and she pressed her forehead to the door when she saw Santigo through the privacy window.

She was still dressed in her shirt from the day and not much else. The shirt hung open to reveal black underthings, but Sophia shrugged and opened the door anyway.

Tigo's gorgeously set features softened into a sensual appraisal. "So glad I didn't bring up those two reporters who tried to bribe me for access."

"Hmph, only two?" Sophia rolled her eyes and left the door open for him to walk through.

"Yeah, the rest decided to bribe security." He grinned and leaned back against the closed door. "This is some town," he added.

"It's somethin', all right," she grunted.

Tigo set down the bag he'd been carrying and opened his arms to offer a hug. Sophia happily indulged.

"It'll be all right." His voice was a soothing balm.

Sophia moaned over its mellow affects. "Promise me that."

"I promise you that." He dropped a kiss on her ear.

Content, Sophia snuggled deeper into the embrace. "I forgot what a good hugger you are."

He chuckled. "So are you." His wide palms folded over her bottom and he squeezed.

Sophia could feel his arousal beneath the wheat-colored trousers as he turned her back against the door in one deft move.

"Mmm…déjà vu," Sophia murmured during the lazy thrusts of their tongues. "I think you tried this move already." She drowsily recalled the events of their previous evening.

"Do you know you talk too much?"

She giggled. "I'm a cop."

"Will you arrest me if I shut you up?"

"I could see you in handcuffs."

Kissing intensified, and Tigo's hand found its way inside her panties. Sophia was instantly affected by the sweet, deep plunge that dipped and rotated before withdrawing to trace the folds of her sex. The moisture he stirred inside her body coated his fingers and produced the most provocatively sensual sounds. Though her hands were weak and she was more interested in winding her hips in response to the love his fingers were making to her, she tried to pull him out of his clothes.

"Why are you wearing a coat?"

"How long since you've been outside?"

"Not since that damn meeting." Sophia shuddered.

Tigo laughed and pulled away to jerk out of the lightweight overcoat. "It's gone from cool to freezing out there."

"And I didn't even offer you a cup of tea." She pretended to pout while curving her fingers into his open collar and tugging him closer.

"I'll let you make it up to me."

Sophia nuzzled her face into his throat. "Promise me that."

He held the side of her face. "I promise you that." He put her up high against the door again.

Tigo shifted his stance and his foot nudged the bag he'd brought up with him.

Sophia smiled at the sound of the crinkling plastic. "Is that what I think it is?"

"Déjà vu again. I brought Chinese." Tigo smiled at the delighted shriek she gave. "There's only one more decision you need to make today."

"No…" She let her forehead rest on his shoulder. "My decision-making skills have been for crap today, Tig."

"I promise it'll be an easy one." He rubbed one of her curls between his thumb and forefinger. "Would you like your Chinese before, after or during sex?"

"How about before, after *and* during?" Sophia shivered deeply when Tigo displayed an effortless show of strength, keeping her high against him and taking the bag of food in his free hand.

He nodded satisfactorily. "Your decision-making skills are definitely improving, Detective."

"That's *chief* of detectives," she purred.

"Now I know what a hooker feels like," Sophia said.

"I think you're exaggerating now."

Sophia grimaced while working her chopsticks deeper into the half-filled pint of shrimp and broccoli. They'd indulged in a delicious mountain of Chinese food before sex, had a wicked session with sweet biscuits and fortune cookies during and were in the afterglow as they finished off the last of the feast.

"You weren't there today, Tig. I felt like an idiot standing around while they positioned me for the camera and talked about me like I wasn't there."

"So what you really meant to say was that now you know what a porn star feels like?"

Sophia bumped her foot against his thigh and then she smiled. "Lem said a lot was riding on me."

"Lem?" Tigo queried.

"Captain of my style team. He said the city needed me and that my image will give the people a sense of faith in the local government blah, blah, blah..." She stabbed at a piece of broccoli. "I mean, why me? I'm not the mayor or the commish. That's *their* job. I'm only the chief of Ds, and I'm not even qualified to hold *that* job."

"Hell, Soap." Tigo set aside what remained of the quart of veggie fried rice, relieved Sophia of her food and pulled her to straddle his lap.

"It's one thing to question *their* motives, but don't question your own ability."

"It's just—"

"Hush."

"Tigo wait, wait please." She brushed her fingers across his mouth. "Now Cole and Hertz will get a trial date any day. No matter how much gloss they slather on it, it won't be enough to blind people into believing all is well. Those two and the other cops we arrested weren't the only ones involved." She bit her lip and debated over her next words.

"Say it." Tigo easily read her hesitation.

"How will it look to 'the people' if I sit up in some office looking pretty while all this is still going on?"

Tigo rested his head against the pillows lining the board. "The job doesn't mean you can't investigate."

Her almond-shaped eyes narrowed. "Do you really think they'll give me time for that?"

"Make time."

Sophia searched the dark soulful depths of his gaze, looking for anything to give her a grasp on his true feelings. She still couldn't accept that he'd revamped his entire outlook toward her job. She focused in on where her nails traced the seductive eight-pack of abs.

"What if *making time* puts me on the street?" She saw the muscles bunch slightly beneath her touch and knew that she had struck a nerve.

"You do what you have to do."

She smiled at his tight response. "And how do you feel about that?"

"I'm fine with it." He took her jaw in his hand, tilting up her head until her gray eyes met his ebony ones. "I'm fine with it."

"That's easy for you to say now because nothing's happening and you're counting on it staying that way."

"I think it's time to shut you up again."

Sophia resisted as best she could when he moved to settle her beneath him. "We'll have to face this sooner or later, Tig. We haven't even talked about the way we left things."

He rolled his eyes, jaw muscles clenching repeatedly. "Why discuss it? It's in the past."

"But I'm still a cop."

"Damn, Soap, how many times will you remind me of that?"

"Does being made aware of it upset you?" She gasped when he suddenly put her on her back.

"What's upsetting me is this conversation, and I'd like to change the subject."

Sophia wasn't done, but Tigo had other plans for her mouth. He kept her immobile beneath him, kissing her as if starved while he jerked away the sheets twisted about their bodies. When she would have tugged out of the kiss, he tangled a hand into her hair and kept her still. His unoccupied hand found her under the covers, and his fingers worked her thoroughly until his name was the only word on her lips.

Chapter 7

Sophia celebrated her foresight in asking Officer Alvin Keele and his partner to meet her at Mathers. While the out-of-the-way bar and grill was frequented by much of the city's blue-collar workers, it was thankfully void of cops and, more thankfully, void of the media.

She'd made the mistake of asking herself how anything could top her previous day from hell. That day answered her question. After morning fashion tips and a complete breakfast courtesy of her nutritionist, she was bustled off to town hall for a series of meetings concluding with the all-important press conference for the city's broadcast media.

Sophia could at least commend herself on doing a reasonably better job in front of the cameras that day. There was even a measure of satisfaction in store when she made it clear that she had no intention of spending her days behind a desk. She was a cop first.

That small declaration had succeeded in rousing a soft

cough from Commissioner Meeks. Sophia wore a more genuine smile for the remainder of the conference.

She walked into the smoky, conversation-filled eatery. In
spite of the hour, the place boasted a pretty packed house. It
appealed to the schedules of workers who toiled all hours of
the day and night. Sophia caught the owner's eye and went
to speak to him.

Drew Mathers's round olive-toned face always appeared
gruff, but everyone knew him to be an easygoing soul. A lazy
grin tugged at his plump lips when he saw Sophia.

"Congrats, Chief," he greeted.

"Not so loud, I don't want to scare off your customers."

Drew laughed and squeezed Sophia's hand across the bar.
"I think two of your colleagues are waiting in one of the
back booths."

Sophia looked in the direction Drew nodded and saw
Alvin Keele and a woman she didn't recognize. She noticed
that they were both in plain clothes. Shaking her head, she
slid Drew a grin.

"Good eye. What gives us away? Do we smell funny or
something?" she asked while removing her quarter-length
overcoat.

Drew kept wiping down the spotless bar as he chuckled.
"No way, Chief. That's a civilian's secret."

"Fair enough." She laughed and glanced back at her coworkers. "What are they drinkin'?"

"Beer."

"Keep 'em comin'."

Alvin stood slightly when he spotted Sophia, but she
waved for him to sit. She slid into the booth beside him and
smiled at the woman she assumed was his partner.

"Detective, *Chief* of Detectives Sophia Hail, this is my
partner, Officer Elzbeta Croft."

"Congratulations, ma'am." Elzbeta reached across the
table to shake hands with Sophia.

"Yeah, Chief, a lot of people are happy about this change."

Sophia winced. "Not so sure about that, Alvin."

"It's true, ma'am," Elzbeta piped up. "A lot of us on the force are starved for superiors who actually give a damn about working and closing cases instead of just putting in hours to secure their pensions."

"Well, that may be true." Sophia sat back against the worn leather of the booth as a server arrived with the beer she'd ordered for herself and the two officers. "I've gotten more than a few nasty looks since the close of the case, though."

She gave Alvin a sideways glance before looking back at the young woman across the booth. "Are you sure about attaching yourself to this investigation, Officer?"

"Yes, ma'am." Elzbeta's words were as firm as the nod she gave.

Satisfied, Sophia produced the bulging interoffice envelope she'd brought with her and set it on the table. "This contains all my notes from the case. I've got good reason to suspect that there are more people who should be going down with Waymon Cole and our former chief of Ds, Paul Hertz." Sophia scratched at her brow and gazed skeptically at the envelope. "Maybe there's something I overlooked in all this. A fresh pair of eyes would be helpful now given my new responsibilities. If you guys find a lead, or even *half* a lead, that'd be great."

Alvin and Elzbeta were already looking through the envelope's contents.

"How far do you want us to take this, Chief?" Alvin asked.

"Not so far that anyone gets a whiff of you." Sophia sipped at her beer. "If other cops are involved, we're gonna have to play it all more carefully than before." She studied the officers covertly while their heads were bent over the notes.

"Are you two really sure about coming on board with this?" she asked again. "You won't even get a pay raise out of it and you'll still have your own workloads to handle."

"Elz?" Alvin traded a look with his partner.

"I hope to be in this line of work for a long time, Chief." Elzbeta's short dark hair framed a face that radiated a delicacy and innocence, yet her small green eyes snapped with a determined fire. "The force means a lot to me. Seeing it tarnished makes me sick to my stomach."

"Ditto" was Alvin's simple reply.

The group laughed and made room for the pitcher of beer the waitress brought then.

"How do we let you know what we've found?" Elz asked.

"We'll switch it up." Sophia closed her menu. "Mathers is great, but we don't want to make a habit out of it. I may give one of you a call, a text or an email, or send a note with your morning donut." She smiled and returned to studying the menu.

"I don't want to get into a routine with anything," she said once their food orders had been taken to the kitchen. "You guys are free to flesh out leads on your own, but take *no* chances." Jamming up two rookies was the last thing she wanted on her conscience.

"We'll be careful, Chief." Alvin raised his glass in a toast. "We're all gonna see this thing to the end."

The threesome clinked their mugs and drank heartily.

Sophia had gone straight home following her dinner with Alvin and Elzbeta the night before. She didn't call Santigo and didn't expect for him to pay her a surprise visit, either. She tried not to think of the way they'd left things when they'd last seen each other.

Tigo hadn't given her any leave for an in-depth chat. They'd spent the rest of the night making love and he'd been gone when she'd woken that next morning. To take things at face value, all was well, and while Tigo's bedroom manner was beyond stunning, Sophia knew her mention of their past troubles was what had truly stoked the fire of the scene.

At least she had the answer to one question, she thought while taking the elevator to her soon-to-be-*ex* office that morning, Santigo Rodriguez had not completely revamped his opinions toward her profession.

The tension she'd sensed in the bull pen seemed noticeably lighter that day. Still, Sophia kept her gaze straight ahead and her pace was determined as she moved deeper into the area. When she heard the first strains of applause, it took some time before she realized it was directed her way.

Regardless, she was still uncertain whether the clapping was a pretense or genuine.

"Congratulations, Chief." Detective Jofi Eames provided confirmation when his hand came down on her shoulder and squeezed.

"Are you serious?" Sophia blurted. Barely half the people in that room had looked her way since the Cole case had broken.

Jofi grinned as if he understood her reluctance to believe in the sudden change of heart. "Even though many of us are closed-minded and set in our ways, we believe in giving credit where credit is due."

"O...kay..." Sophia extended the slow reply and then gave an even slower nod to the applauders.

A few stepped forward to begin the handshakes. Polite to a fault, Sophia accepted them graciously. The tension dipped several additional notches as more colleagues came forward with handshakes, hugs and well wishes or a combination of all.

Lieutenant Glenn Arnold rounded out the well wishes when he, too, approached to commend Sophia.

"Did you have anything to do with this?" she asked when they exchanged a brief embrace.

"Me? Nah..." Glenn chuckled and then sobered. "I wish I could take credit for having such power over a gang of cops, but it's like Jof said. We give credit where credit is due."

"Sophie!"

Sophia, Glenn and Jofi all turned to see Sergeant Laine Deeds approaching.

"Congratulations on the promotion, hon. Hey! Love the suit." Laine stepped back to admire the walnut-brown pantsuit with a coordinating tan silk blouse beneath; the cuffs peaked out stylishly from the short blazer.

"Thanks, but my style team gets all the credit." She waved a hand when her colleagues appeared dazed. "It's a long story."

"Well, that's one I want to hear—" Laine cast a quick look over her shoulder "—but you've got a courier waiting in your office."

"Oh." Sophia glanced at her watch. "Thanks, Laine. I better go see to it. See you guys later." She waved or nodded at others who passed her en route to her office.

"Sorry about the wait," she said to the courier, who had taken one of the chairs before the desk in the room.

"Sounds like a party," the man noted while handing Sophia the receipt pad when she reached for it.

"Well, I was definitely surprised." Sophia smirked while signing for the item and then exchanged the pad for the package. The man stood.

"Thanks." She tore into the padded manila envelope.

"You be careful, Chief. Very careful." He left the room.

Sophia was searching the envelope when the courier's words registered. Clarity hit in unison with her discovery that the package was empty. She dropped it as though it burned to the touch. Quickly, she covered the short distance to her door, seeking out the courier. If he was near, he'd already blended into the sea of bodies swelling the bull pen.

She looked back toward the empty envelope.

"This is too much," Sophia breathed.

The lanky brown-skinned man standing next to Sophia offered a hearty chuckle. He mopped sweat from his face with the dingy handkerchief he'd taken from the front pocket of his tan work shirt.

"Standard-issue," he said.

"*This* is standard?" Sophia was incredulous as she ogled the sleek black Dodge Charger with chrome rims, tinted windows and plush black suede interior.

"Standard issue for the new chief of Ds," Harold Mackey clarified.

"Well, I never saw Paul Hertz drivin' around in any souped-up piece of eye candy."

"Yeah…guess you're right." Harold stroked his stubbled chin while he considered Sophia's argument. "Hertz was humble enough to drive his own car. What was it? A Jag? No, no, a Mercedes, right? So humble, that guy."

"All right, all right, you made your point." Sophia rolled her eyes.

"Accept some of the job's fringes, kid. You've earned 'em. No one's gonna hold it against you."

"You may be wrong about that."

"Now, Sophie—"

"I think somebody just threatened me, Harold."

"You sure?" The head mechanic for the Philadelphia Police Department was serious.

"I think so." Sophia massaged her neck. "I mean, why would he tell me to be careful. *Very* careful? A delivery guy? He doesn't know me well enough to say something like that."

"Maybe he watches the news." Harold shrugged at her sour look. "Did anybody recognize him?"

Sophia shook her head and leaned against the hood of her new "standard-issue." "Laine says she saw him in the office but didn't talk to him, just noticed the uniform and stuff."

"And I guess you didn't get a good look, either?" Harold leaned next to Sophia on the car.

"Damn it." She worked her fist into her palm while cursing her carelessness. "I didn't look at all. He had his back to me when I walked in the room. I was focused on the pad and the package…"

"Which was empty?"

"Empty." Sophia hid her face in her hands. "Stupid…thank God it was empty and not filled with—"

"Now, look, stop." Harold half turned toward her on the car. "Stop feelin' sorry for yourself and go talk to somebody about getting a protective detail on you."

"Right," Sophia agreed, all the while cringing over the idea. A protective detail would have her parents even more difficult to handle.

And then there was Santigo. Something told her that after their previous evening together, he'd be even less concerned with hiding his true feelings over the way she earned her living.

"Tell somebody, Sophie," Harold stressed the point as if he sensed she was warring with herself over whether or not to do so.

"You know better than anyone that you ain't dealing with folks who play by the rules."

"I know that." She raked her fingers through her hair and inhaled the aroma of oil and machinery within the garage. She laughed then. "I can see myself now going everywhere with my style team and security entourage, ha! That'll go over well with the taxpayers."

"It'll go over a damn sight better than the taxpayers losin' a second high-ranking member of the P.D. in less than a month."

Once more, Sophia nodded and sighed. "Right."

"So wait a minute, what'd this fool do while you were out handlin' business? Cooped up in the club…taking inventory?"

The two couples at the wide round table drew several

glances from both sexes as they conversed and laughed bois-
terously. Elias Joss and Clarissa David had recently returned
from the first leg of their trip surveying the Jazzy B's Gentleman's Club franchise left to Clarissa following her aunt
Jazmina Beaumont's passing.

Clarissa used the end of a red linen napkin to dab a tear
from the corner of her eye once laughter quieted over Santigo's comment. "Actually, I was the one who spent most of
the time cooped up in the club."

Tigo's mouth curved downward in a gesture to show that
he was impressed. "Nice," he said.

The foursome erupted into another roar of laughter. The
group had planned a dinner out once Eli and Clarissa had
returned and gotten settled in from the trip.

"Elias was the one out and about meeting with the crews,"
Clarissa explained of her increasingly significant other. The
Jazzy B's franchise was in the midst of a full-scale remodel-
ing project that Joss Construction was overseeing.

"Everything still okay with everything?" Tigo asked before sipping from his mug of beer.

"No complaints as far as the construction goes...."

The comment had Tigo's and Sophia's brows rising, after
which they traded looks.

Clarissa looked toward Eli. "I'm thinking of turning over
all management to Rayelle." She referred to Rayelle Keats,
her aunt's right hand and Clarissa's closest friend.

"Well, I can't think of a better person for the job." Sophia
pulled apart the roll she held. "You'd know there was someone looking out for the club's *best* interests."

There was no need for clarification on Sophia's meaning.
It was Rayelle's sharp eye that had led them to the discovery
of the cryptic journal that put Sophia onto Waymon Cole's
scent and the corruption he'd allowed to infiltrate the club.

"How's the case going?" Clarissa asked.

"Mr. Cole wants a deal."

"Will he get it?" Elias asked.

Sophia smiled grimly. "I'm working to see that he doesn't."

Eli nodded. "Was Mr. Cleve any more help?"

"He gave us a lot more information on other cops involved," Sophia shared. Cleveland Echols was a man both Elias and Tigo had known since they were children. "We think Mr. Cole wants to deal with someone higher up the ladder. Mr. Echols just didn't have the information to shed light on that particular area. There were plans for his network of banks to headline things, but when he got cold feet it seems they started having second thoughts about sharing information that might clue him in on the *real* players in the mess."

"That's a lot on your plate, girl." Clarissa rested her chin on her palm after she put an elbow on the table.

Sophia nodded. "But I've got help, two rookies looking back over my notes from the case. Maybe fresh eyes can find something my tired ones overlooked." She sighed, leaning back in her chair. She intentionally avoided the probing stare Tigo sent her way.

"Have you seen your new office yet?" Clarissa asked. "I remember how small the one is that you've got now. It'll be nice to have more room, huh?"

"Very." Sophia folded her arms across the front of the powder-blue cashmere sweater she wore. "I've seen my office *and* my new car."

Elias whistled.

"I could do without it all, though," Sophia said in spite of her grin.

"Well, you've done a great job." Clarissa squeezed her wrist. "There's no shame in enjoying the benefits."

Once more Sophia nodded. All the while she thought that she could live with the benefits. It was the threats she was having trouble with.

The waiter arrived for their dessert orders. Afterward, Eli whisked Clarissa away to dance. He told her they probably wouldn't be able to move after the dessert course anyway. They left Tigo and Sophia at the table, where silence reigned for a while.

"What's wrong?" Tigo asked finally.

Sophia knew it'd be unwise to put on a happy face, but she wasn't about to divulge the full truth. She toyed with the thin gold chain above the scooping neck of her sweater. "It's just been a long day, Tig. The new car was a lot to deal with."

She cleared her throat and reached for her wineglass. Again, she avoided eye contact. She didn't need to look his way to know he was giving her one of his all-knowing looks. The kind that told her he knew she was giving him a load of bull.

"So how was work today?"

"Why?" she blurted.

Tigo uttered a short sound that masqueraded as laughter. He brought an elbow to the table and studied his hand for a time. "I'm trying here, babe. You have to know that."

Sophia studied the soulful obsidian of his gaze and nodded. "I know that, Tig. I, um…I think I was threatened today."

The "What?" he whispered chilled her, but she knew he'd heard.

"I'm not sure—"

"Sure enough, though?"

She took a deep swallow of her white wine and waited for the inevitable explosion.

"What are you gonna do about it?"

Her head jerked up. She was clearly stunned by the question.

"I know I should tell someone."

"And you're considering *not* telling someone. Why?"

"I just…" She shook her head and turned suspicious eyes on him. "Why are you being so calm about this?"

He smiled and looked down as he tugged on the lapel of his chestnut-brown sport coat. "It's the whole turning over a new leaf thing, yada, yada…" His expression had hardened by the time he looked at her again. "Don't misunderstand me here, Soap. I'm pissed as hell over this and at you for thinkin' about not telling me."

"I just hate to make an issue of it," she confessed, tapping her nails against the stem of the wineglass. "If it turns out to be nothing, everyone will think I'm paranoid and even *less* qualified to have the job. *Also*," she added before he could break in. "Also keeping quiet might draw out whoever's behind it."

"Hell, Sophia." Tigo caught his hand in a fist and closed his eyes as if to rein in his emotions. "Are you stupid enough to use yourself as bait?"

Sophia let her expression serve as an answer.

Tigo let a more flagrant curse fly as he dragged all ten fingers through his dark waves and tugged.

"I think whoever's behind this *threat* is part of the crew Waymon Cole is trying to rest his deal on."

"And you actually think this plan of yours is sound?" Tigo spread his hands out flat and studied her incredulously. "I get why you can't make a deal with the snake, but putting your ass on the line is idiocy."

"My ass was on the line when I broke the case, Tig. I may as well go all the way, right?"

"Jesus…" He massaged his forehead and then grabbed Sophia's hand. "I just got you back," he spoke into her palm. "I don't plan on losin' you, not ever. Do you understand what I mean?"

She scooted over into Clarissa's chair and held his face in her hands. "I do." She kissed his mouth. "I do." She let her kiss linger.

Chapter 8

"So these guys are in jail for stealing a car that was already stolen?" D.A. Paula Starker asked Sophia after they'd met in a downtown park for coffee one chilly morning. "How do you know this?"

"My rookie cops scored." Sophia warmed her hands around the paper mug. "Found it in some papers Laureen Bradford passed along."

Paula sipped at her coffee in a studious manner and then pinched a corner from the cinnamon Danish wrapped in pastry tissue. She was about to pop the food into her mouth but hesitated. "Did the kids know who the car belonged to?"

"It was registered to Greenway Construction so…" She shrugged beneath her leather jacket.

"So these kids just *happen* upon a stolen truck? What do those odds look like to you?"

Sophia grimaced. "Extraordinary as hell." She sent Paula a sideways glance. "You're gonna have to let their public defender know. Think the guys'll talk then? One of 'em works for Greenway. You think he'd be a little pissed that his boss hasn't looked into having the charges dropped."

Paula brought the cup to her mouth but didn't sip. "You'd think…" She changed her mind about sipping from the cup. "Have your rookies turned up anything else?"

Sophia shook her head and leaned over to rest her elbows on jean-clad knees. "But they're vested—determined to see this put to bed."

"And how are you and Santigo?" Paula asked after a few conversationless moments. "Are you still buying his reformed act?"

"I don't think it's an act, Pauly."

"Well, well." Paula looked impressed. "If I didn't know better, I'd swear the man's willing to do anything to get you back."

"No." Sophia smiled thoughtfully. "Not anything. He won't lie to me about being okay with it all."

"How can you be sure of that?" Paula snuggled into her black cashmere sweater and warmed her hands on her cup.

Sophia appeared to be measuring her response. "I think I was threatened a few days ago. I told Tig and he wasn't too happy about it or the fact that I'd thought of not telling him."

"Threatened?" Paula was obviously stunned.

Sophia waved a hand. "It was nothing."

"You're insane."

"I can handle it."

Paula was already digging out her phone.

"What are you doing?" Sophia watched the woman activate the touch screen.

"What the hell do you think? I'm putting someone on your skinny tail."

"Don't." Sophia snatched the phone. "I want to keep this quiet a little longer."

"You *are* insane," Paula whispered.

"They'll expect me to put on a protection detail, Pauly.

I'll throw them off by *not* doing that. The more unpredictable I am, the more dangerous I am."

"And the more urgent it'll be to shut you up. Permanently."

Sophia flopped back against the cool wooden bench. "You're not a cop. You don't get how important this is. One bad cop puts a stain on the whole force, and we had a helluva lot more than one."

"It's still not your job to try and clean up the mess on your own." Paula faced her on the bench.

"I'm the one who discovered there was a mess to begin with, remember?"

"I give up." Paula drank heavily from her coffee cup. "Do what you want. You will anyway." She raised an index finger. "But don't expect the people who care about you to just stand by and do nothing to keep you safe. Remember when *one* cop puts a stain on the force we need as many *good* cops as possible to clean up the mess." She tipped her cup to Sophia in a mock salute.

"She's still a good look for you," Elias noted while signing papers left by his assistant Desmond Wallace to review upon his return from the trip with Clarissa.

"Thanks, but this is something I already know." Tigo smirked.

"I see." Elias's focus was still on the paperwork. "And did you know this back when you let her walk away from you?"

Tigo laughed then. "Bravo, man, still got that talent for bringin' a person straight down."

Elias grinned.

"And I didn't *let* Sophia walk away." Tigo went to the bar in the corner of the office. "She did that all on her own."

"But you didn't do anything to stop her, did you?" Eli pulled his blue stare from the papers when Tigo set a bottle on the wood-grained bar top with more force than needed.

"You sure about putting yourself through this again? She's still a cop, just one with more rank now."

"Only thing I'm sure of is I can't do without her."

"Come on." Eli feigned disbelief. "You're the most successful ladies' man I know."

"Hmph." Tigo poured a drink. "Not hard to be successful when what you're after is hollow."

Eli maintained his disbelief. "Are you trying to tell me you're after some kind of commitment from the girl?"

"You offend me, El. I've always wanted a commitment from her."

"She know you still hate her job with a passion or is she still buying your reformed act?"

Tigo downed the shot of whiskey he'd poured and grimaced at the burn filtering through his throat. "She saw through it right away." He joined in when Eli laughed.

"Case sounds like it's far from over." Elias returned to the papers he'd been signing. "She's still dedicated to solving all of it. You ready for the situation that could put her in?"

"Hell no." Tigo's reply came without hesitation.

Eli watched his friend more closely. "Pour me one, too," he said when Tigo helped himself to another shot.

Tigo obliged and handed Eli the drink while claiming his preferred seat along the edge of the desk.

"Her job still scares the hell out of me, but I get that to have her I have to accept *it.* Doesn't mean I can't do everything in my power to keep her safe."

Eli was studying the light flooding the glass of amber-colored liquid. "What's that mean?"

Tigo savored the whiskey burn with more relish that time. "I've got folks working to get answers about Carl and Lester's boys."

Eli frowned a moment and then nodded as he recalled what Tigo had told him earlier that morning about the boy's legal troubles.

"I'm sure I can tug somebody's sleeve about keeping an eye on her, too."

"Be careful, man." Eli downed his shot. "Don't step too far into that. Sophie doesn't look like the type to take kindly to her man questioning her ability to do her job."

Tigo watched his hand as he clenched it in and out of a fist. "It's not her ability I question, but what others might do to keep her from doing her job at all."

"Harold, I swear you can trust me. I haven't put one dent on the car." Sophia laughed when she walked into the spacious yet cluttered office of the P.D.'s chief mechanic.

"As much as I love you, you don't need to waste your time calling me in for weekly checkups."

Harold Mackey tried and failed to keep a forced smile in place.

"Everything okay?" Sophia caught his look.

"Shut the door, Sophia."

Quickly, Sophia pushed closed the wooden door with its glass-top window. She perched on a table loaded with car parts closest to where Harold sat behind his desk.

"You're scaring me, Harold."

Harold focused on the path his index finger traced across the oil- and coffee-splattered desk calendar. "The boys that got pinched in that traffic stop. Why were you interested in that?"

Sophia recalled what she'd told Harold about the carjacking. She'd wanted to assure him that she had more going on than the Cole matter. "My parents are friends with the parents of one of the boys."

Harold's nod was solemn. "Last thing I wanna do is put you in harm's way, girl."

"It's my job, Harold."

"And one bull's-eye on your back is enough, and this is definitely bull's-eye material."

Sophia inclined her head. "This is about the Cole case?"

"No, but this issue with those boys seems to have teeth of its own."

Sophia narrowed her eyes in a half playful, half suspicious manner. "You ready to be a detective again?"

Harold glared at her. "When I left to work down here, I never looked back. But I'm still a cop, too, and this has a stink about it that'll probably lead back to more of our brothers in blue."

Sophia eased off the table and down into a folding metal chair. "Harold, what are you talking about?"

He looked past the windows framing the office, satisfied that the floor appeared empty.

"Did you know the truck they were charged with stealing was registered to Greenway Construction, who one of the boys works for?"

"Yeah, the rookies helping me investigate put it together."

Harold's nod was somber. "And you knew the truck had already been reported stolen before those kids were ever stopped in it?"

It was Sophia's turn to nod somberly. "None of it makes sense."

Harold swiveled his desk chair restlessly. "That truck got sent to the impound while the boys were booked. I got a call from a friend who works over there." He reached for something on the table behind the desk.

"This is a picture of what they found during the inventory."

Sophia gasped once she'd focused on the screen of the phone Harold held. "Where?"

"Panel beneath the truck's flatbed. Ernest said he almost fell through it while he was moving around back there during inventory."

"How much is it?" Sophia eyed the picture on the phone

that showed neat blocks of bills stacked high beneath the truck's flatbed.

"One hundred and eighty-five K."

Sophia whistled. "Wonder if the guys knew?"

Harold set the phone to his desk. "Hard to say, but I hope they were smarter than to drive around in a work truck owned by the folks they stole from. Smart thing to do would've been to switch out the cash."

"If they knew it was there…damn it. You know this could be nothing." She cast a skeptical eye toward the phone. "Maybe Greenway just doesn't trust banks." She gave a doubtful smile.

"Well, there's more you should know before you go with that train of thought. Two cops came askin' about the truck the very night it got there."

"Did your friend know them?"

"He didn't but says his gut told him they were rookies."

"Hell…" Sophia eased her hands beneath her hair and began to massage her neck.

"You trust these rookies on your team?"

Sophia thought for a moment and then gave a firm singular nod to solidify her assurance. "Did your friend get the cops' names?"

"They hurried out once Ernie put 'em off about procedure and waiting on paperwork for the truck. He told 'em to come back in a few days and then he called me. We moved it here to the garage. We should be able to keep a lid on it for a few more days."

"The owner might ask," Sophia warned.

Harold stabbed a finger at the desk calendar. "Then he best be prepared to answer a few questions, as well."

"Depending on who else is involved, our questions may be swept under a rug."

"So what're you gonna do, Detective?" Harold asked after they'd sat quietly for a few moments.

Sophia slouched in the chair. "My dad knows Sylvester Greenway. I've always known him to be an upstanding guy… but I really don't want to go to my dad with this."

"You say your parents are friends with the kids' folks. Maybe your dad's already tried to reach out. You could ask."

The idea made Sophia shudder. Given what had happened at the Reed House dinner, she didn't want to put her parents in the middle of another mess, especially if the claims were unfounded. "I'll talk to the D.A. first," Sophia decided. "Get an idea of how she wants to move forward from here."

"You trust her?"

"Yeah, I do. She's gonna be one of the good ones, Harold."

"Ain't many of those." Harold smiled faintly.

Sophia reciprocated the gesture. "There're not many of those at all."

"Coming to see me?" Sophia happily assumed when she ran into Tigo on her way back into the precinct following lunch.

Tigo pulled her into a telling embrace, exercising little care for whoever may've been watching. He was actually there to see Jofi Eames but knew he could talk to the detective later about what more he may've found on the Roche-Bradford case.

"Going or coming?" he asked, patting her hip beneath the hem of the sandalwood blouse she wore under a lightweight coat.

"Coming back from lunch."

"Ah…and did you use it to eat or to work?"

"A little of both. Good enough?"

Tigo's broad shoulders rose beneath his beige suede jacket. "It's an improvement."

Sophia laughed. "I promise to get better at it. Any chance to roll around in my new car is worth it."

"And when do I get the chance to…roll around in it?" He nuzzled her ear.

"Funny you should ask that." She bit her bottom lip when he stepped back to watch her.

"Do we need privacy for this conversation?" His smile was cunning.

Sophia observed their surroundings. They stood on the busy steps leading into the precinct, but no one appeared very interested in them.

"The commissioner is planning some event to celebrate changes on the force and my new post."

"Changes on the force?"

"I'm clueless." She slapped her arms to her sides. "So would you mind being my arm candy to this thing if it happens?"

"You know I don't mind." He tilted his head to look more directly into her eyes. "Why do I feel like you were on the fence about asking me?"

"No, I—"

"Soap."

"I don't want to assume too much too fast, all right?"

"Are you the same woman I've been sleeping with?

"Yeah." She smiled. "Yeah, that's me."

Tigo didn't seem convinced that all was well, but he decided not to push. Not there.

"So do I have to wait for the commish's party to get a ride?"

She shook her key ring. "I'm a public servant. Your destination is my command."

"Well, then." He eased an arm beneath the coat and around her waist.

"Careful, man," warned a passing detective. "The lady carries a gun."

"So will you take me anywhere I ask?" Tigo queried once they were done laughing over the teasing precaution.

Sophia pressed herself in closer against his chest. "Anywhere."

"My bed?"

"Hmm…not sure the car will fit in the elevator, but as your public servant it's my job to try."

"I like your dedication to the task at hand."

She shivered as he nuzzled her ear with greater intensity. "I can promise you it gets better."

"So what was it about the truck that made you suspicious?" Officer Alvin Keele asked from his end of the sofa.

The man on the other side of the couch was having a hard time looking his academy classmate in the eyes. He paid more attention to picking at the tufts of cotton peeking out from tears in the worn fabric.

Elzbeta Croft shifted a look to her partner and then leaned closer to the man who sat nearest her. "Hey, Rick, take it easy. It's just the three of us. You're not in any trouble."

"Says you," Officer Rick Jessup grunted. His sandy-red hair stood on end as a result of incessantly running his fingers through it.

"Is somebody givin' you a hard time about the stop?" Alvin asked.

Rick rolled his bloodshot brown eyes back toward the sofa's stuffing. "Let's just say I've had a lot of folks…inquiring."

"Are they giving you a hard time?" Elzbeta asked.

Rick mussed his hair. "Not exactly, not on the surface."

"But you can tell something's up?" Alvin watched Rick nod his bowed head.

"Rick, tell us what happened that night."

"It was a good stop." The young officer looked Elzbeta in the eye. "Everything was by the book. There was nothin' racial about it. We saw a big truck cruising near the vicinity of a nice neighborhood. First thing we think is they're casing for a job. I ran the plates and didn't really expect to find anything, but when the damn thing came up stolen…" He dug the heels of his hands into his eyes. "I flashed the lights—had no idea what I was gonna do. I think I was more scared than those kids, both me and Lance were." He referenced his partner, Lance Southern. "And I swear we didn't know they were black till I walked up to the driver's side of the truck."

"What sort of flack have you been getting?" Alvin asked.

"We swear we aren't here to make trouble for you," Elz encouraged.

Rick surveyed his colleagues with weighty looks and then nodded. "You guys remember the cops they took down over that Waymon Cole thing? They didn't even clear out half the dirty ones—just made room for more. You know how hard it is to be good when they're bribin' you to be bad?" He directed the question to Elzbeta and then looked to Alvin. "You know."

Alvin nodded. "We're better than that, man."

"That's hard to believe when you're being recruited to the dark side by your own instructor."

Elzbeta blinked, curls bobbing as she swung a loaded look in Alvin's direction.

"They asked me about the truck," Rick said. "Asked if I looked inside, if the kids said anything to make me think *they'd* looked inside…."

"Did *they* tell you what was inside?"

Rick massaged his rough jaw and shook his head. "But I'd bet whatever my badge is worth that it was cash and those poor kids I busted were the patsies."

Tigo was totally enjoying his inaugural ride in Sophia's new vehicle. His dark, remarkable stare traveled a leisurely trail across her shapely mahogany-toned legs and thighs bared by the rise of her skirt's uneven hem.

Reaching across the gearshift, Tigo brushed the back of

his hand across her knee and then rubbed the material between his fingers. "Is this standard cop attire?"

Sophia angled her head and smiled. "Lem and the others say folks want to see a tough, capable cop who's also secure enough to embrace her femininity."

"Ahh…" He eased back more of the skirt's hem, baring more of Sophia's thigh. "I think you can assure them that you definitely embrace it."

"Hmph, but why do *I* have to prove that? Paul Hertz never had to prove his masculinity."

Santigo was still enjoying the view beneath Sophia's hemline. "Guess it's meant to show people how different you both are."

She pulled to a stop before the light and lowered the volume a bit more under the vintage slow jam that spilled from the car's state-of-the-art speakers.

"I think they're trying to keep people's minds off what's going on behind the scenes."

"Diversion," Tigo guessed, falling for that very tactic when he raised the skirt's hem high enough to see the lacy edge of her panties above the lacy tops of her stockings.

Sophia observed his actions with a raised brow. "I guess some are just fine with me being a sex object."

Tigo lifted his gaze and smiled wickedly. "Do you mean me?" He shifted a bit in the passenger seat to face her more directly. "Would you arrest me if I admitted that?"

Sophia's laughter filled the car's dark mellow interior as she pulled into the underground parking lot of the high-rise complex Tigo called home.

"Do you have some fantasy about me handcuffing you or something?"

"I've got lots of fantasies where you're concerned." He sobered and took his hand from her skirt. "Right now, I'll settle for the truth, though."

Sophia blinked, unsettled by the sudden topic change.

"Why were you second-guessing asking me to the thing with the commish?"

"Tig." She placed her forehead against the steering wheel. "It's like I said—I just don't want to assume too much too soon."

"Why?" He leaned his head back on the rest. "We were almost on our way to the altar once, remember?"

"But we didn't make it there, did we, T?" She made a hasty exit from the car.

Tigo was out of his side and blocking her escape before she even heard the door slam. He said nothing, and Sophia knew he was silently commanding her to finish. She leaned against the trunk and studied the toes of her platform pumps. "I feel like there's this big, invisible…other shoe that's hanging over our heads and waiting to drop."

The harsh look confining his beautifully crafted features melted and he moved in to brace his hands on either side of her along the trunk. "Afraid I'm gonna need you to explain that one, Chief."

"Me being on the fence about the party was about not wanting to put it out there that we're a couple and then having to publicly deal with all the looks and whispers when—"

"We don't work again," he finished.

He'd bowed his head, and Sophia could see the flex of muscle at his jawbone.

"Maybe we shouldn't talk about it now," she suggested.

"We pushed it aside long enough." He looked up at her. "When it's all said and done, the fact is that you don't trust me anymore."

"That's not true." Moisture made her eyes glisten.

"You're afraid I'll walk away again."

Despite the tears blurring her gaze, she smiled. "I think you're forgetting that *I'm* the one who walked away."

"Because I made you."

"I honestly don't want to talk about this." She blinked

quickly to dash the water from her lashes. "I don't want to talk at all."

Santigo appreciated the support of the car while he rested his hands on the trunk. His body's reaction to Sophia had begun to cool—barely—but it churned right back up to a boil at the words she uttered.

She pushed off the trunk and snuggled into him. "Can't we forget it? Least for tonight?" She tugged the ends of the silk tie he'd loosened during the drive.

"You were on your way to work when I ran into you." His baritone voice was quiet, and his hands curled into fists against the car as she began a merciless assault on his earlobe.

Sophia bit down into the soft flesh as if to punish him for the reminder. "You don't expect me to believe you had me drive us all the way over here to let me just turn around and leave with nothing to show for my time, do you?"

"What have you got in mind?" His hand had already disappeared once more beneath the hem of her skirt.

Sophia curved her fingers into his suit coat. She felt him inside her panties, his thumb fondling her clit. She gasped when two of his fingers invaded her sex. "I'm positive you'll think of something."

Chapter 9

"Are there cameras in here?" Sophia asked as she and Tigo ascended in the elevator to his apartment, which occupied the top two floors of the building.

Chuckling, Tigo barely raised his head from Sophia's cleavage. "We're shit out of luck if there are. I'd say the film crew's already gotten their money's worth out of us."

The elevator's chrome doors glided open silently. Tigo pulled Sophia behind him and out into the apartment's sunken living room.

"Whoa. Business must be good," she commented, observing the relaxing masculine surroundings. The gray, black and burgundy color scheme was soothing in tone and aura. The living room was simply furnished, and oh-so-comfortable burgundy sofas sat on either side of a plush gray rug that covered over half the room's hardwood flooring. Deep black armchairs occupied one end of the rug. The chairs faced a gorgeous black lacquer-framed fireplace. Stout burgundy-shaded lamps with wide gray bases doused the room in a golden glow. She turned at the sound of Tigo tossing his keys into a dish on the credenza behind the chairs.

"Yeah, we do all right for a group of troublemakers."

"Tsk, tsk. So harsh. I don't think Eli would appreciate that label." She pulled off her jacket and holster. "Looks like he was the only sane voice among your group of rugged thugs."

Tigo chuckled while nodding his agreement. "That may be true. Even *I* have to admit the guy's advice is sound."

She walked off to trail her fingers along the back of one of the sofas. "Have you partaken of any lately?" She froze when the full force of the view hit her. Philadelphia laid spread before her eyes beneath cloudy late-afternoon skies, which drew the eye to the lights from neighboring scrapers.

"He told me I'd be a fool to try and have you protected."

When she looked at him, he shrugged and eased the undone tie from his collar. "You already know my attitude adjustment was a fake. If it was up to me, I'd have had a security detail on you the first day you left the academy."

"Paula wanted to do just that when I told her about the threat."

"Does that mean we're still the only two who know about it?"

"I told Harold Mackey—he's the department's chief mechanic." She flinched when Tigo's vicious curse darkened the room.

"Do you even trust *any* of your brothers and sisters in blue?"

Her smile was sad. "Not many."

The words broke Tigo's heart. He watched her return to enjoy the view and allowed her less than a minute before he closed the space separating them. Then, he was jerking her into a kiss.

Sophia's hunger for him, which never settled, fired up intensely, and she threw herself into the act. Eagerly, she curved an arm about his neck and sank her fingers into his dark hair.

Her free hand tugged insistently at the shirt tucked just inside his trousers. Once she'd freed it, her fingers were quick to undo the buttons. Sophia only managed to loosen Tigo's belt before he sank to the sofa and tugged her astride his lap.

Greedily, she began to strip him of the shirt, when he pressed his forehead to her chest and held it there.

"Tig? What is it?"

He offered up no response, and Sophia discovered that she really didn't need him to.

"I'm okay," she whispered, kissing the top of his head and nuzzling her face into the soft crop of ebony curls. "I'm fine. I'll *be* fine. I'm a cop who's been taking care of herself for a long time."

Suddenly, Tigo switched gears and put Sophia on her back beneath him. "You're gonna have to excuse me if I don't seem to agree that you should be doing that."

Sophia opened her mouth to speak, but she couldn't seem to find the words. No matter. His tongue was filling her mouth and she happily lost all focus.

Not so for Tigo. His focus was sharper than ever. Every thrust of his tongue into her mouth reminded him of how sweet she was. Sophia moaned, arching herself into him when he settled in snug at her center. Tigo cupped her hips, and he could only focus on how pliant, how soft she felt beneath his hands. Nothing that was so alluring, so provocative to the touch could be strong enough to handle threats and corruption, he thought. A subtle voice told him that was a crock and he knew that. Of course it was his sensible side that registered the truth, but just then he was more in tune with the sexist, arrogant side of his psyche that bellowed otherwise.

Sophia could feel her heart in her throat, placed there by a mix of excitement over what was being done to her and how. Her breathing came in ragged pants, slightly labored, and she shivered, giving in once more to that feminine side of herself. She was all too ready to lose herself in the strength of his embrace.

Tigo had already unbuttoned the flirty yet professional blouse she'd teased him in since he'd first seen her that day. He took care of the buttons lining the skirt in the same fashion as her blouse. His hormones hummed their satisfaction at the glimpse he caught of the front-clasp bra she wore. His deft touch rendered the clasp a memory seconds later.

He was parting the satiny cups to bare the pert chocolaty-brown mounds to his ravenous gaze. For a time, Tigo took pleasure in simply outlining the full, softly scented orbs by using the tip of his nose. He drew his hands over her hips, cupping her bottom still wrapped in the folds of her skirt.

Again, Sophia lost her fingers in the luxurious thickness of his hair. She tried to direct his mouth to her nipples, which were budded and aching for him.

Tigo ignored her plea but placated her with gentle nips to her flesh as his nose trekked around the darker cloud of skin surrounding one nipple. He tightened his hold on her when she moved in sensual frustration as though starved for more than he was giving her.

His warning squeeze had Sophia curling all ten of her fingers into his hair and tousling it in agitation. She bit down on her bottom lip and expelled a shudder when he at last took one nipple into his mouth. The other, he subjected to a maddening succession of rubs and squeezes that sent her wriggling restlessly beneath him once more. Moans and breathy sighs escaped her lips in a stream of shameless arousal.

Tigo was groaning as well, feeling his sex throb and tighten ever more in response to the feel of the nipple grazing his tongue. When he moved on, Sophia cried out her disapproval and thumped his shoulder with her fist.

"Hey," he complained. "That's police brutality."

"I promise you I'm capable of more."

He continued to kiss his way down her body. "Take you up on it later. You're doing enough right now, thank you."

She moaned. "Will you ever let me use *any* real energy around you?"

"I'll think about it."

Her lashes fluttered apart at the feel of his breath on her thigh. Coming out of her haze somewhat, she discovered that he'd eased down the length of the long sofa to the part of her that was wet for him. He kissed her through the damp middle of her panties, and her thighs shook.

Slipping a hand beneath each of the trembling limbs, Tigo held her secure and continued pecking at the moistened center of her panties. Sophia circled her hips, pushing vague thrusts against his mouth. Tigo glided cotton kisses into the dip of her inner thigh and chuckled when Sophia threaded five fingers through his hair to put his head—his mouth—back to where she wanted.

"Police brutality," he sang once more.

"Sue me."

"I prefer other things."

The wordplay trailed off and he was curving a hand into the waistband of her panties, yanking them downward.

"My shoes." The pumps were a gorgeous creation of the same sandalwood color as her blouse. A leather strap and buckle were secured over each trim ankle.

Tigo observed them thoughtfully as he pushed himself up to complete the journey of gliding the panties along her calves. "Leave 'em," he smirked.

Sophia wanted to assist in the disrobing and moved to finish undoing Tigo's trousers. He brushed away her hand and returned to his spot at the juncture of her thighs. His thumbs stimulating her clit, Tigo inhaled her fragrance while trailing his nose up and down the silky folds of her sex. His free hand hooked over her thigh once more and drew it farther away to allow himself more room to play.

"Tigo…put your mouth there…" she purred when he finally began to make love to her with his tongue and lips. She worked her hips in time to the plundering strokes invading her core.

Tigo felt the telltale tremble and knew she wouldn't last much longer. "Stay with me, babe."

Breathless from arousal and amusement over his playful arrogance, she laughed. There was more grumbling from Tigo's end and then a growling sound emerged from deep and he gathered her closer. The intimate exploration of his tongue deepened and he would not stop even as she cried out and drove herself against him in the grips of a potent climax.

Santiago could hear her begging him still. Her voice was quiet as though she hadn't the strength to summon more volume. He understood her frustration, understood that her senses were stretched between exhaustion and satisfaction. Knowing that he was the catalyst to her reaction was yet another favorable nudge against the more sexist side of his nature.

Once Sophia lay fulfilled, he showed mercy. As exhaustion claimed her consciousness, he rested his head on her thigh. His contentment over her response to his touch coaxed him into a deep slumber.

Sophia awakened in bed—Tigo's bed. She squinted to make out more of her surroundings. The room was almost dark save the light streaming in weakly beneath the closed master bathroom door, and she wondered how many hours they had spent there.

The thought sent her whipping back the covers and feeling around for her clothes. After a few unsuccessful moments of clothes searching and then hunting for a light switch, Sophia made her way to the bathroom door. Pushing it open, she was greeted by a rush of steam.

Tigo was just shutting off the water when she padded into

the large black-tiled bath. The realization of what he was up to caused Sophia to halt her steps. She didn't want to miss the sight of him leaving the shower.

A few minutes ticked by before he sensed her presence. Sophia couldn't have been more pleased as it gave her time to observe him unaware. Thick wavy locks matted to his head in rows of drenched black, while water rivulets streamed down his defined chest to join the dark curls surrounding the magnificently crafted endowment below his waist.

Santigo pushed hair off his forehead and then pinched his nose to drain water from his nostrils before he looked up. Ebony eyes brightened when they settled on Sophia.

"Hey."

The inviting deep hush of his voice caused Sophia to shiver.

"Did I wake you up while I was in here?" He rubbed the towel through his hair.

"No." It took her a moment to snap to. "Um, I didn't mean to fall asleep."

"But you need it." He walked toward her. "You could use a little more." He tilted back her head to study her closer.

She lowered her eyes. "I'll sleep more when I'm home. Promise." She flashed him a quick glance and smiled.

"Why home?" He took her elbows and led her to the long gray marble counter that occupied a far wall.

"I, um." She ordered her eyes off the thick length of his sex. "I just, uh—tomorrow's a busy day." Her lashes grew weighty with need.

"Why home?" he asked again, clearly making note that he didn't believe her. Slowly, he toyed with her disarrayed curls, drawing them away from her hair in order to gnaw at her neck then tongue-kiss her ear.

"Tig." Her intention was to set him back when she laid her palms on his chest. Instead, she became awed by the chords of water-slicked caramel-toned muscle beneath her fingertips.

He moved in, spreading her thighs and taking his place between them. He tugged until her bottom was near the very edge of the countertop. One hand cupped her waist, the other her hip; all the while he tongued her ear.

"I should go." The words were spoken without a shred of sincerity.

"You can't leave me like this," he spoke next to her ear and nudged her with the erection that had been consistently firming since he'd set eyes on her after his shower.

"Tigo…"

"Come on…you being my public servant and all—it's sort of your duty, you know?"

She shuddered, eyes fluttering closed as delight surged throughout her body at the feel of his wide sex at her entrance demanding the treasures inside. Sophia melted, grasping his hair and drawing him in for a kiss.

The act was rough and lusty, yet somehow Sophia managed to ease back a little.

"Tig, I—I'm not using anything," she warned softly when the broad rim of his shaft eased forward just barely.

Tigo covered her neck beneath his hand and smiled at what he saw in her eyes. He plied her with a kiss that was hungry, throaty, possessive…

Sophia knew she should have been a mere puddle on the counter by then. She was just as hungry for him as his kiss proved he was hungry for her. The kiss became more than a ravenous melding of their tongues; it was a declaration of need and exquisite consummation.

He was cupping her bottom, unconsciously positioning her to receive him when she cautioned him again. He muttered something and, weakened by desire for her, rested his head on her shoulder. After a few moments in the vulnerable position, he opened a drawer beneath the counter and rooted around inside. He tossed several condom packets into the black porcelain sink nearest them.

Sophia would have laughed, but his kiss snuffed out her ability to do so. She gave herself over to the rising sensations. Linking her arms around his neck, she left it to him to handle the rest.

Tigo approached the task with great zeal. Efficiently he put protection in place and tugged her thighs, drawing her to him. Sophia threw back her head when she felt him slide into her. Would she ever tire of the feeling? she wondered, wrapping her legs around his still-water-slicked back.

The force of Santigo's kiss may have snapped her neck had Sophia not reciprocated just as powerfully. His tongue thrusts against hers and gravel-laced groans of satisfaction kept time to his rocking hips during the rediscovery of her charm.

Next, it was Tigo ending the kiss to rain pecks across her collarbone and the swells of her bouncing breasts. His legs were weakened by the passionate romp, and he braced a hand on the long mirror at Sophia's back to steady himself. Somehow he increased the power behind the seductive drives of his hips.

Sophia was miles away from finished, yet she didn't begrudge him when she felt the steady pulse of his sex inside hers as he spent himself inside the condom.

"Sorry." He shuddered again, laying his gorgeous face on her shoulder.

Sophia's eyes narrowed to twin almond-shaped slits. "Are you serious?"

He chuckled even as he appeared somewhat abashed by her teasing scold. Summoning the strength to move, he kissed her cheek and withdrew. "Grab a shower. Dinner'll be ready by the time you're done."

Sophia stayed where she was, watching as he cleaned up and left the bath. Content, she remained on the counter for a while longer and hugged herself.

* * *

A simple shrimp and vegetable stir-fry over rice was enjoyed before the fire less than an hour later.

"Mmm…I still can't believe it's already cold enough for a fire." Sophia, garbed in one of Tigo's old T-shirts, curled in closer on the oversize chair they shared.

"I'm ready for an early winter. Only time of year I feel like bein' in the kitchen."

"Yay winter…" Sophia drawled, using her fork to stab a chunk of shrimp and carrot from the plate she and Tigo shared.

"Cooking's no fun when it's only done for one." He grimaced.

"You're so right." She voiced the agreement even though the words made her stomach muscles seize. "Luckily I don't have the time to cook—even for one."

Tigo held the plate dutifully, though he'd lost interest in eating. "Maybe you need someone to do the cooking for you."

She giggled. "Why, Santigo Damien Rodriguez, are you offering to be my personal cook?"

"No. I'm offering to be your husband."

Sophia's fork hit the shared plate with a clatter that rang out like a clash of cymbals. She opened her mouth, but sound wasn't forthcoming.

Tigo set the plate on the coffee table. He remained hunched over, elbows on his knees, while he worked his jaw muscles before he looked at her again.

Sophia had never been so happy to hear the distinctive chiming of her phone than at that very moment. She scrambled off the chair to grab it from an end table before the call went to voice mail. She could feel Santigo's stare fixed her way and intentionally kept her back turned. She answered the phone, having to greet Paula Starker more than once since the woman was in the process of telling someone that she didn't want any bull crap.

"Why the hell are you out of breath?" Paula asked once she'd joined the conversation.

Sophia glanced at Tigo, who was in the process of clearing the coffee table of their dinner items.

"What is it, Paula?"

"Just wanted you to know we've got a meeting with your ex-boss in the morning."

"Paul?" Sophia blinked. With effort, she pulled her eyes from Tigo, admiring the way the navy sleep pants rode low on his hips as he left the living room.

"The one and only," Paula confirmed. "Detective Hertz requested a meeting. He and his lawyer with you and me."

"Why me?" Sophia asked.

"Who gives a damn?" Paula scoffed. "The man's been in jail almost two weeks—no bail, no nothing. He and Cole have good attorneys and they're still there, which means someone wants them there. Someone way up high. Maybe Hertz has had enough and is ready to spill his guts. His only request for doing so is that you be there."

"Right, right." Sophia mussed her hair and nodded. "I'll be there."

Paula rattled off the details of the meeting and then ended the call as unceremoniously as she'd started it. Sophia studied the phone once the connection had dropped. Her attention was pulled toward the kitchen, where she could hear what sounded like an exaggerated clatter of dishes.

With a sigh of dread, she tugged at the hem of the T-shirt and set off to find Tigo. In the kitchen, she cleared her throat, but he made no effort to acknowledge her presence while raking the last of the meal into the disposal.

"That was work." She hooked a thumb across her shoulder.

He was quiet a while longer and then coughed out an ill-humored laugh. "Isn't it always?" His tone was beyond gruff.

Sophia's resigned smile proved that she hadn't expected a better response. "Guess it's finally time to go."

When he continued to work with the dishes and give her the silent treatment, Sophia took heed of the pressure behind her eyes and knew tears were at hand. Before they could emerge, she turned and left the kitchen. Blindly, she stumbled to the bedroom, sniffling and swiping at the tears that would not remain at bay.

"You're a cop, you're a cop," she softly reminded herself in an effort to solidify the fact that she was too tough to dissolve into a quivering mess just because Tigo had hurt her feelings.

She jerked out of his shirt and stomped around the room in her panties while she looked for her clothes.

"The rest of your stuff is still on the couch."

She stiffened at the sound of his voice. Reclaiming the discarded T-shirt, she made for the door, but Tigo refused to let her leave when she got there.

"Do you have to go?" he asked.

"I have a meeting."

"Tonight?"

"In the morning."

"Then stay."

"Tig—"

"I'm done talkin', Soap."

She blinked, gray eyes harboring skepticism as they studied his very appealing features.

"Will you stay with me?" He smiled and then glanced briefly past her shoulder. "I promise you won't wake up to find yourself strapped to my bed."

The mere threat made her want to moan. She swallowed. "You don't want to talk about—"

He tugged away the shirt she held to her chest and helped himself to a lengthy scan of her bare form. "I promise that talking is the last thing I want to do with you."

Chapter 10

Sophia feared her very nutritional breakfast would reappear when she saw Detective Paul Hertz waiting obediently for his meeting with her and Paula the next morning. She felt ill, watching the once-vibrant, in-control leader appear as a shell of the man she once knew, now dressed in the baggy orange jumpsuit adorned with chains for foot restraints and handcuffs.

"We'll be ready in a second."

Sophia didn't turn at the sound of Paula's voice. She wasn't so sure about the *ready* part. That was no surprise, of course. She hadn't been sure of much since Tigo's proposal the night before.

It was a proposal, wasn't it? *Idiot.* She rolled her eyes in spite of herself. Was she a bigger idiot for not recognizing a proposal or for recognizing it and not accepting? Sophia postponed her answer when she heard a male voice joining Paula. She turned.

"Chief of Detectives Sophia Hail, this is Detective Hertz's chief counsel, Thom Geary."

"Chief Hail, it's a pleasure," the shorter solid man greeted with a handshake and a smile as glum as his dull blue gaze.

Sophia nodded. "Mr. Geary."

"Chief, I must reiterate my extreme concerns about this meeting. I'm completely against my client speaking with either of you." He slid a look in the D.A.'s direction.

"Look, Thom, your client called *us* in case that tidbit slipped your mind."

"And my team and I have done everything we can think of to get him to reconsider."

Paula threw up her hands. "So are we gonna do this or stand around yappin' about it all day?"

Thom pursed his already thin lips and gave Paula a chilly once-over. "Follow me."

Sophia hesitated, taking a deep breath before she followed the grim duo.

Former chief of detectives Paul Hertz stood the moment his eyes connected with Sophia's in the uninviting concrete interrogation room. The chains binding his waist and ankles jerked him back down to his seat before he rose too far.

Sophia cleared her throat as emotion filled it with an unyielding lump.

"Thanks for coming, Sophie," he said when she was able to look his way again. "Thank you both." He sent a humble glance in Paula's direction.

"Detective, I have to say that I'm forced to agree with your counsel here." Paula shifted a look toward Thom Geary. "This meeting could potentially place you in an even tighter spot than you're already in."

"I understand, Ms. Starker."

Thom Geary cleared his throat noisily. "Whatever is said in this room will be completely off the record. We'll debate the details of obtaining a more formal statement later."

Paula rolled her eyes but nodded her agreement. She slapped her hands on the sides of her black pin-striped skirt. "So, Detective, what are we doing here?"

Paul Hertz looked at Sophia again. "I am sorry." He tapped his fingers together as he spoke. "I never set out to dirty the uniform. Once I made that first step…I just…couldn't help myself. The money…" He closed his eyes. "We never dreamed of making that much, and then came the job of having to hide it."

"Takes a lot of interested and powerful parties to hide that kind of money." Sophia's voice was soft and nonjudgmental.

"Yeah." Paul shook his head. "We thought we had that part figured out until Cleve Echols had his crisis of conscience. Waymon must've suspected that he would because he didn't skip a beat when Echols flaked out on the deal for the new bank. Cole already had plans for a new site, even a new construction company to handle the project for us."

Sophia frowned while leaning back in the thinly cushioned metal chair she'd taken across from Paul.

"So are we here because you'd like to shed light on the identity of *us?*" Paula asked.

"Ms. Starker, this is bigger than either me or Waymon." Paul dragged his fingers through his dark blond hair and kept them there for a time. "The biggest part of money laundering is transporting it, and transporting it in such a way so as not to be discovered. Doing that effectively has as much to do with the how as the who."

"Would you mind dumbing that down for us?" Paula sighed. "What exactly are you trying to say?"

"Be careful, Paul," Thom Geary cautioned his client.

"Henry Fields," Paul answered before a second had passed.

"He's an instructor at the academy, right?" Sophia rested her elbows on the table.

Paul twisted his mouth. "That's the one."

"But why?" Paula's bewilderment was momentary. "To get them fresh off the tree," she guessed.

"That was the idea." Paul nodded. "Not only were they fresh and loyal, they were ambitious. The more ambitious, the better. Those kids weren't stupid." He leaned back, folding his arms across his middle. "They knew there were cops out there who retired to cushy lives with more than their pensions to show for it."

Sophia massaged her temples. "You guys are monsters."

Paul shifted uncomfortably in the chair and nervously traced invisible patterns on the stainless steel table.

Paula tapped her pen on the portfolio she'd been scribbling notes in. "So you and Cole along with Detectives Cana, Franks, Coria and Seitman." She named the others who had been arrested to that point. "You all took part in the laundering—"

"Off the record, Starker."

"Keep your boxers on, Thom." Paula didn't make eye contact with the attorney. "So, Detective, you all took part in the laundering using yet-to-be-named rookie cops to transport the money. Who are they?"

"I swear I don't know that part." Hertz spread his hands palms-up on the table. "The scam worked so well because each side had its own role to play. Cole wanted me to get the transporters, so I contacted Fields at the academy to get me some fresh—" he cursed himself then "—fresh meat," he finished. "I never met them. You'll have to chat with Detective Cana for the names."

Sophia cursed then and pushed her chair noisily away from the table before she stood and walked away.

"Heard enough?" Thom Geary asked Paula.

"Is there more?" Paula propped her chin on the palm of her hand and shrugged. "'Cause it sounds like all your client has to offer is someone even further down the pole than he is."

"I'm not looking to skate past a prison term, Ms. Starker."

"Paul—"

"Shut up." Paul Hertz appeared a shade of his former self when he snapped the order to his counsel. He looked to Sophia, whose back was still turned on the table.

"You know what they'll do to me in jail, Soph." His voice cracked. "I'm only asking to be put someplace where I won't wind up dead my first night inside."

"That's not asking for much," Thom Geary told the D.A. on behalf of his client. "He's already been threatened upwards of ten times since he's been here. We've been working our asses off to get him out of here, meeting brick walls of bureaucracy at every turn."

Sophia had turned and was observing Paul Hertz's gaunt, whiskered face. His healthy tan had paled and emphasized the shiner around his left eye.

"We'll talk," Paula told Geary as she stood to collect her things. "I'll see what I can do about the accommodations," she told the defamed detective in a gruff but soft tone of voice.

At Paula's nod, Sophia made her way toward the interrogation room door. She halted before she cleared the table and leaned over to squeeze her colleague's hand before she exited without a look back.

"Pathetic," Paula noted once they were in the outer observation room.

"Why'd you go soft on him in there?" Sophia studied the square toes of the stylish black boots peeking out from the legs of her wine-colored trousers.

"He's looking at a healthy sentence." Paula rolled her eyes. "Healthier still if all he's got to bring to the table is a police academy instructor. Doesn't hurt to give him a little hope, even if it *is* false. Besides—" she secured the strap of a leather tote across her shoulder "—he's looking for shelter someplace where they don't kill shamed cops. I'm not sure such a place exists for ones who've ratted out their fellow brothers in blue." She shrugged her brows and set off. "I'll catch you later."

Sophia remained in the corridor, watching Paul Hertz and his attorney through the one-way mirror.

Sophia returned the wave that Clarissa David sent her way from across the dining room at the bar and grill where they'd arranged to have an early lunch.

"Sorry I'm late." Sophia leaned over to hug Clarissa when she got to the table.

"Stop." Clarissa waved a hand. "If anyone deserves to be running a little behind, it's you." She got more comfortable on her side of the cushioned booth. "From the looks of things, you're gonna be a very busy lady for a long time."

"Yeah…"

The melancholy response triggered Clarissa's curiosity, but the waitress arrived for Sophia's drink order before she could inquire. Once the woman walked away, Clarissa reached over to pat Sophia's hand.

"Honey, are you o—"

"Tigo proposed," Sophia blurted.

"Kay…" Clarissa sighed the rest of the question, turned acknowledgment. Her mouth formed an O.

Sophia put her head down on the table and then looked up and gave it a quick toss. "At least I *think* he did."

"I guess it's safe to say that you didn't respond with a 'Yes, Tigo, yes'?"

Sophia rolled her eyes toward the table as though she longed to rest her head there again. "I was too shocked to say anything at first, and then I got a call about work."

The waitress returned with Sophia's iced tea and to take their food orders.

"Could we have a few more minutes?" Clarissa smiled and nodded at the server when she complied. "So how'd you leave it with him?" she asked.

"I wanted to go home." Sophia spoke in a disdainful tone as if she was ashamed of the admission. "He asked me to stay at his place—promised that we wouldn't talk about it… the proposal." She set an elbow on the table and stirred her tea with a straw.

"He was already up when I woke this morning. I heard him in his office on the phone with business." Her expression took on a more miserable tint. "I left before he was done."

"Sophia…" Clarissa trailed off with a sympathetic smile.

"Go on and say it." Sophia took a quick swig from the straw before setting the glass back on the red oak table. "I'm a coward and a horrible significant other."

Clarissa laughed and raked a few fingers through the chic short cut she sported. "I'm afraid you're asking the wrong person. I'm not experienced enough in the 'significant other' role to judge you on that." Work had pretty much been Clarissa's "main squeeze" for as long as she could remember. That is, until she'd lost her heart and her virginity to Elias Joss.

"As for being a coward…" Clarissa toyed with the wide cuffs of her blouse. "I think it makes sense to be a little scared. This is marriage you're talking about. You've only been back together for half a minute, right?"

"I wanted to say yes."

Clarissa smiled. "'Course you did. You love him."

"So what's wrong with me?"

Sipping at her lemonade, Clarissa twisted her lips over the tartness of the drink. "I think you already know."

Sophia blinked, her dark face registering acceptance. "Tig is lying to himself." Her gray eyes surveyed the crowded dining room. "He thinks he's suddenly developed this 'enlightened tolerance' for my career." She rolled her eyes back to Clarissa.

"He hasn't, and part of him knows that but he—" She shook her head at the craziness of it all. "He still believes he's got more than he had before. He thinks it's enough for us to last this time."

The waitress arrived for her second attempt at taking food requests.

"Go on and order if you're ready." Sophia flopped back against the booth.

"Club sandwich with fries, please." Clarissa slid Sophia a wink. "We can share." She thanked the waitress and tapped Sophia's arm when they were alone again.

"How do you feel about all this?"

Sophia rested her head against the seat and focused her gaze on the lamplights lining the walls of the cozy, dim establishment. "I honestly think I'll go out of my mind if we don't make it this time."

Clarissa squeezed Sophia's hand reassuringly. Sophia squeezed back.

"I'm trying so hard not to get too used to him, too pampered by the idea of us together again. It'll be too hard when it all ends, and it will once Tig starts being honest with himself."

Eli's long brows rose over his striking sky-blue stare when he walked into his partner's office and heard the man laughing. He was about to retreat, but Tigo waved him inside. Elias waited until the call was done. It concluded with Tigo telling the person on the other end that it was great and to keep him posted.

Tigo rapped his knuckles along the walnut finish of his desktop when he shut off the phone.

"Can you share?" Eli asked.

"That was Carl Roche. Looks like the lawyers I put on the kid's case are confident the judge will grant 'em bail."

"Mmm..."

Tigo observed Eli stroking his jaw in a show of concentration.

"What?"

"Wouldn't it be better if the charges were dropped altogether?" Eli asked.

Tigo laughed. "Well, hell yeah, it would, but I'll take a *little* good news over none any day." The ease of his expression drained and was refilled with something darker. "Somethin's gotta work out today." He followed the grim acknowledgment by shoving a sheaf of papers to the floor.

Eli watched the pages drift down in a flurry. "Sorry for putting down your headway in the case."

"You're good, man. My mood's just been in the crapper all day."

"I see." Eli rested his massive frame against the closed office door and hid his hands in his pockets. "Anything worth talkin' about?"

Tigo swiveled his chair to and fro for a few silent moments. "I sort of asked Sophie to marry me," he confirmed finally.

The ease of Elias's stance against the door was completely at odds with the shock he was feeling just then. "Oh, um… could you explain the *sort of* part?"

"Wasn't anything like what it was supposed to be." Tigo picked up a bit more speed in the chair's swivels. "Nowhere in the hemisphere of being suave. I just said that I'd like to be her husband."

Elias knew he had to tread carefully. One look at Tigo's face was enough of a hint to warn how wildly his emotions were raging. "What'd she say to that?"

"I didn't push for an answer." Tigo looked to be on the verge of a smirk. "I think she was too stunned to give me one, and *I* was too afraid she'd say no."

"Aw, man, don't be so pessimistic. She said yes before, right?"

"I never actually asked before." Santigo winced at the admission. "It was the obvious road we were heading down, but I never said the words."

Eli studied the lines in his palms and chose his next words carefully. "Did you mean it when you *sort of* asked her? Dumb question," he said, spying the harsh look Tigo sliced him. "So? Now what?"

"Anybody's guess." Tigo pushed out of the chair to collect the papers he'd shoved off the desk. "I'll call…see if she wants to grab dinner. If I get the brush-off—" he let the papers settle back on the floor "—guess I'll have my answer."

After lunch with Clarissa, Sophia returned to the precinct in time to meet with Alvin and Elzbeta regarding the Bradford-Roche case. She celebrated her decision to put the two rookie officers on the job. With everything going on with her new job and the Cole case, she hadn't spent as much time focused on the boys as she should have.

She and her investigators had communicated by text and email so she'd been able to share what she'd uncovered from her discussion with Harold Mackey.

"What have we got?" Sophia asked the officers. They'd met outside a conference room down the fluorescent-lit hall from the bull pen. "What?" she queried at the look Alvin traded with Elzbeta.

"We have a witness who says Ian Roche and Ken Bradford were used as scapegoats."

Sophia stepped back. "Who's the witness?"

"Rookie cop, Rick Jessup," Elzbeta said. "He told us he was…approached at the academy."

Sucking in breath, Sophia mopped her hand over her face. Her earlier suspicions during the chat with Paul Hertz had been dead-on, she realized.

"Did the rookie give you a name?" she asked suddenly, training the clear gray pools of her eyes toward Alvin. She could see confirmation to the questions in Alvin's thin, attractive face.

"Henry Fields."

Sophia let him see her regret.

Alvin raised a hand, knowing the concern was due to the fact that the respected instructor was his girlfriend's father.

Sophia nodded, folding her arms over the short blazer she sported and studying Alvin for any sign of weariness. She smiled at the resolve she saw on the young man's face.

"So where's our star witness?" she asked.

Elzbeta hooked a thumb across her shoulder while the other hand rested over the gun belt at the waist of her uniform. "We've got him waiting in the conference room."

Sophia blinked. "He's ready to talk?"

"Seems that way." Alvin shrugged. "He feels bad about what he's done, Chief. This wasn't the kind of cop he set out to be."

Bowing her head, Sophia recalled what Paul Hertz had said about the rookie's being fresh and loyal. *Right, Paul, but you and your friends underestimated how loyal they'd be to the badge.*

"Either of you ever sit in on an interview?" When the officers shook their heads in a simultaneous and eager fashion, Sophia waved them on ahead, smiling when Alvin and Elzbeta bumped fists in triumph.

Her phone chimed before she could fall in step behind the younger cops. Sophia hesitated to answer when she saw Tigo's name on the faceplate.

You're no coward, she reminded herself. "Tig?" She appreciated the airy quality of her voice on answering the call.

"Are you okay?"

Damn it. Would his voice always stop her that way? she wondered. The warm depth of his tone was like a blanket. All she wanted was to curl up and forget everything. "I'm fine. I— Tig, I'm sorry for how I left this morning." She cleared her throat when emotion threatened to stifle more words. "You sounded busy on the phone, and I had a meeting."

"Your style team?"

She laughed at his guess. "I wouldn't put it past them to come looking for me if I wasn't home when they got there."

"Will you meet me later?" he asked once a brief bout of crisp silence had held the line.

"My place or yours?" She assumed without hesitation or any intention of refusal.

"May be better if we go out this time."

"Right." Her heart was in her throat and all she could do was wait for it to return to its place. She let his choice of words sink in as well, and reminded herself once again that she was no coward. "I'd like that," she lied.

Tigo gave her the time and place and then told her he loved her. He severed the phone connection before Sophia could offer any reply.

Chapter 11

Sophia returned to her office following the meeting with Officer Rick Jessup. The young policeman confirmed the suspicions that had stirred as Paul Hertz shared his tale of woe earlier that morning.

Alvin and Elzbeta were eager to know of their next move. Sophia instructed them to keep digging. Back in her old office, she left a message for Paula to call her. They had to brainstorm on how to handle this latest wave of information. Afterward, she clicked on the battered thirteen-inch TV still perched on an even more battered metal filing cabinet. With the midday news for company, Sophia adjusted the volume on the television and went about browsing the last of her things to be packed away.

She was halfway through a hoard of papers found tucked away in the bottom of a desk drawer when the phone rang. She was expecting Paula, but it was her mother's number on the phone screen.

"You're no coward, Sophie," she reminded herself for the

third time that day. "Hey, Mama," she greeted in her cheeriest tone.

"Hey, baby," an equally cheery Veronica Hail responded.

"Sounds like you're having a good day." Sophia went back to riffling through her old papers.

"Things are definitely looking up."

"Can you talk about it?" Sophia leaned over to drop a few items into the wastebasket.

"Looks like Laureen's son will be getting out of jail soon."

Sophia forgot about shuffling through old paperwork then. "Are you serious?"

"Mmm-hmm," was Veronica's perky response before she laughed. "I was sure you would've heard by now. Sounds like that judge had a change of heart. Honey?" Veronica queried when Sophia had gone silent for several moments.

"Did Miss Laur say when this would happen?" Sophia had hoped she could speak with the boys' attorneys and encourage them to talk to her once she'd had more evidence regarding their charges.

"She said it could be anytime, and, baby, please thank Santigo when you see him."

"Thank him?" Sophia laughed even as a frown creased her otherwise flawless brow. "What's that about?"

"Well, honey…" It was Veronica's turn to laugh. "Santigo was the one who got the new counsel for Kenny and Ian. He's paying all the boys' legal fees and everything. I'm surprised he didn't tell you."

"Yeah…" Sophia rocked her chair back.

Veronica didn't attempt to quell her curiosity. "So have you seen him lately?"

"I'm having dinner with him tonight, Mama." Sophia had to smile at the woman's poor attempt at slyness. She could practically hear Veronica's applause on the other end.

"Well, you tell that boy that he's done a wonderful thing. Lester and Laureen couldn't be happier."

"I will, Mama, and I'll talk to you later, okay?"

"Honey, before you go, we really do need to discuss the party."

"Party." Sophia's voice was flat.

"The celebration for your promotion."

Sophia rested her forehead against her palm. So much time had passed since any mention had been made of the party. Sophia had hoped her mother had forgotten about it.

"We still need to decide on the guest list, the type of party you want."

"Type?"

"Well, yes, baby. Do you want a dinner party or reception or—"

"Mama, I'm really not interested in any of it."

"Well, that's fine, honey. I'll handle it all."

Sophia massaged the bridge of her nose and wondered whether her mother had intentionally misunderstood.

"Mama, I really don't want any party."

"That's just your nerves talking. Don't worry about it. I'll call you soon with the time and the place. Now you go and have fun with Santigo tonight, you hear?"

"Good grief." Sophia winced when the connection severed. She kicked the desk drawer to air her frustration but only succeeded in making noise when her boot slammed the old metal. She was rubbing tingles of stress from her temples when she noticed the TV screen.

"What the hell?" She'd kept the volume low and groped around on the desk for the remote. She found it lodged in the side of the box she'd been packing.

A minute passed before Sophia understood why Waymon Cole was grinning so broadly on-screen. The reporter covering the story announced that a judge had overturned the decision to deny bail. There was even a sound bite from the judge who'd made the new decision.

Sophia watched as Judge Oswald Stowe discussed the contributions Mr. Cole had made to the community.

"…and he's eager to get started on preparing his defense and the court finds no fault in allowing him the freedom to meet with his counsel as they work to do just that…"

Sophia studied her desk while considering the implications of the latest developments. The broadcast caught her attention again.

"It's been a day of surprising decisions here at city hall. Two young men being held on the charge that they'd stolen a truck from a local construction company are also free on bail. Back to you in the studios, Lee."

Sophia put the TV on Mute and tossed the remote back into the box.

"A personal visit from a judge. Should I contact my lawyer?" Tigo grinned and greeted Judge Reginald Creedy with a handshake when the man arrived in his office that afternoon.

"*You're* fine—I can't say the same for some of my colleagues." Reginald hiked up the legs of his maple-brown trousers before taking a seat on the sofa across the office.

Seriousness registered in Tigo's probing dark eyes. "I know you didn't come all this way to make me guess."

"Judge Oswald Stowe ring a bell?"

"What's up?" Tigo folded his arm over his chest.

"He booted Cole and Hertz out of city hall, then went one better and bounced the kids, too."

"Yeah, I heard about the kids." Tigo strolled over to sit on the arm of the chair flanking the sofa. "Good to know I made the right call getting them more representation."

"Yeah, that was a good move, and I'm sure the new counsel is splendid, but I don't think the thoroughness of their motions had anything to do with the guys' release."

Tigo inclined his head, silently prompting Reg to continue.

The judge sighed, his unease evident. "I think my colleague's on the verge of hanging up his robe."

Tigo moved from the arm of the chair to the chair itself. "How do you know this?"

"Judge's intuition." Reg rubbed his hands together and shook his head slowly. "Those kids were arrested for stealing a truck from Greenway Construction—a company where one of them works—a company that's been on Stowe's Christmas list for years.

"Then for some reason, he denies these kids the get-out-of-jail-free card that everyone else seems to have. And then out of the blue suddenly says yes to their bail."

"And from that you think he's about to call it quits?" Tigo frowned skeptically.

Reg shrugged one beefy shoulder. "Smells like he's cleaning up a mess, tying off loose ends."

"I have my suspicions, but what makes *you* think there's a mess to clean up?"

"Cole has ties to Greenway. They were one of his clients."

Tigo's grin caused his alluring gaze to narrow. "He's allowed to have them as a client, Reg. Are you tryin' to pin every crime in town on the man?"

Reginald grinned slyly. "Sure would make things a lot easier." Some of the amusement drifted out of his expression. "Just doesn't sit right with me is all. I can't help but think my old colleague is afraid somebody's gonna uncover this stink and take him down with all the rest."

Sophia cheered her ability to put together a passably posh outfit for her dinner out with Tigo. She'd been on the verge of calling Lem and the crew for a quick session, but, as her love life was already part of the public record, she decided against it.

She was confident that she'd paid enough attention to her appearance for the evening. She was ready enough for whatever the outcome would be from a night of good food and lighthearted chatter or dramatic discussion and rattled feelings.

Sophia smiled at the host, who made a point of congratulating her on her promotion before telling her that Tigo had just arrived. She followed the man's lead into almost pitch-blackness.

The Island was a restaurant evidently geared toward couples desiring the utmost privacy while they dined. Sophia was glad Tigo hadn't made an issue of picking her up for dinner. She needed as much time as possible to collect her courage.

"Damn it, Soph, stop it," she muttered, flexing her fist as she followed the host into the ever-thickening darkness. They may not even discuss…that.

Sophia was still so withdrawn into her thoughts that she gave a start on realizing that she and the host had arrived at the table. She heard Tigo thanking the man, feeling as if she were standing outside of her body while her date and their host traded light, brief conversation.

Then, she felt Santigo's hands at her waist and the familiar, incredible scent of his cologne drifted past her nostrils. With the host discreetly leaving, Tigo brought her closer to brush a kiss across her temple. Her eyes had not yet adjusted to the virtual darkness, making her more dependent on her other senses.

"Thanks for coming."

Especially her hearing. She could feel his voice vibrating through his broad chest and into her back. Sound and touch made her want to swoon. She resisted the temptation and reined in her reactions a bit too sharply.

"Why wouldn't I have come?" she blurted and winced, thankful for the dim lighting then.

"Well, I proposed to you last night, or did you already forget that?"

So much for not discussing it, Sophia thought, silently

cursing herself for opening that door. Tigo didn't seem to desire a response and simply eased her down into the small booth they would share. Seconds after they'd settled down, a small light illuminated closest to where Tigo was seated.

"Your drink orders, Mr. Rodriguez?" a soft voice inquired.

Tigo pressed the lighted button. "Give us a minute, will you, Kelly?"

Sophia laughed to drown her nerves. "Do they expect us to read a menu in this?" She raised her hands to note the darkness.

Smiling, Tigo tapped at a spot behind her head.

"Oh." Sophia saw an engraved light fixture illuminate beneath his touch.

"Guess you've never been here." He took a drink menu from a wooden slot near his end of the booth.

"No. Guess you have, though."

"Nope. My first time, too."

Sophia prayed the surroundings were still dark enough to hide the sight of her mouth falling open.

No such luck. Tigo chuckled, having spotted her reaction in the dim lighting. "I don't know whether to be flattered or offended."

She made a show of fixing the flared long sleeves of her silvery-blue frock. The bodice was a V-cut that dipped erotically low.

"You *should* feel very flattered, Tig. I hear your social life is a thing most men envy."

"It's nothing to be envious of."

Sophia knew she wasn't imagining the sudden edge in his voice. The bulb in the table glowed again.

"May I take your drink order, Mr. Rodriguez?" Kelly's voice was as soft as it had been on her previous check.

"Do you need more time?"

Oh yeah, he was pissed. Sophia heard the edge turn to downright gravel.

"Um." She leaned toward the bulb. "White wine," she said and listened as Tigo ordered one of the imported beers on the menu before he tossed it on the table.

Sophia was most thankful for the dim lighting then for it hid the sight of her smoothing damp palms on the cushioned embroidered black fabric of the booth's seat.

"We should go on and decide what to eat. They'll be calling back soon." He grunted an ill-humored laugh while passing her a menu. "I'm just assuming it's how they do things here. It's got nothing to do with my many supposed visits here."

"So should we expect our drinks to just suddenly emerge from the middle of the table?" Sophia had regretted her earlier quip about his social life and was trying to lighten the mood.

The tease didn't illicit the hoped-for amused response from Tigo.

"You turned me down last night," he said instead, absently studying the menu.

Sophia shook her head and half turned to face him on the seat. "I didn't turn you down," she whispered.

Tigo snapped his fingers and smiled. "That's right," he whispered. "That's right—you didn't give me an answer at all."

Sophia let her lashes settle to shield her gaze. She summoned the music gods and urged them to let Maxwell's vintage neo-soul piece, "Whenever, Wherever, Whatever," calm her.

Their server at last emerged in the flesh to deliver the drinks. Tigo and Sophia managed civil responses as they placed orders for steak and shrimp entrées with salads to start.

"Is this why you wanted dinner out?" she asked when the server had gone. "You wanted to interrogate me in public?"

"Is that what you think I'm doing?" His voice carried a

frightening ease. "All I've said is that you turned me down. I haven't even asked why."

Sophia bowed her head, inwardly stumbling on a reply. "I haven't thought about why."

His response was a vicious, soft curse.

"I was too surprised that you even proposed at all." She inclined her head. "Why *did* you propose?"

Her perplexed tone sent him slamming a fist into the center of the table. His beer mug, Sophia's wineglass and Sophia herself jumped in response.

"I did it because I love you," he growled.

"But before you—"

"You never gave me the chance to before. You were already bouncing your ass off to that damned precinct of yours."

"You jerk." Sophia pushed a finger into his shoulder through the fabric of the tailored chestnut-brown shirt he wore. "Don't forget *why* I bounced. Remember that nice little ultimatum you gave me, Tig?" She just barely made out his smirk in the dim, and her heart lurched.

"Will you ever forget that?" he asked.

"Why should I? You haven't."

"So why did you turn me down, Soap? Is it my successful social life or your disbelief that I'm trying to accept your job?"

Her hand shook as she reached for her glass and took a sip. "Listen to yourself, Tig." She spoke with a measured calm that surprised her. "I've been a cop for years, and you're still *trying* to accept my job. What happens when you finally admit to yourself that you'll *never* accept it?" She bristled when he leaned in to raise the lights.

"Before I was just guessing and even then I knew it was true." The look that claimed his gorgeous face was equal parts hurt and disbelief. He shook his head as though mesmerized once he'd watched her for a minute. "You really *don't* trust me, do you?" He didn't need a response. He saw the truth in her expression. Bowing his head, he expelled a soft sound akin to laughter but aeons from amusement.

Elbow propped on the table, he set his palm over the mouth of the beer mug, raised it, reconsidered and then put it back down.

"Why've you been sleeping with me if you don't trust me?"

"Tigo, please." Her voice was thick as a sob hung in her throat. "I do trust you."

"To let me in your bed but not into your life, right?"

She opened her mouth, ready to negate what was fact.

"Save it."

The waiter arrived with their salads.

"You can take mine back."

Sophia curled her fingers into his shirtsleeve. "Tigo, please don't do this."

He ignored her and stood. "This should take care of it," he told the short young man while pulling loose bills from his wallet. "And your tip." He pressed the money into the server's shirt pocket on his way past and out of the dining room.

"So I think we should just drop the charges against everyone, let 'em all get home in time for Thanksgiving. What do you say?"

"Sounds good."

Paula rolled her eyes when her second attempt to pull Sophia from her daze went unrewarded. Taking a more drastic route, she grabbed one of the heavy legal encyclopedias from her desk and let it drop to the surface with a boom that succeeded in jerking the detective from her reverie.

"What the hell's wrong with you?" Paula demanded when Sophia only blinked and looked at her blankly.

"Nothing." Sophia rubbed her arms beneath her sweater's metallic-blue cashmere sleeves as if she was chilled. "Where were we?"

"Oh, well, let's see... You just agreed to drop the charges against Cole and his cronies."

"What?"

Paula's wan smile followed a quick toss of her bobbed hair, and she pointed a finger at Sophia. "You'd remember that if you weren't sitting over there being preoccupied by nothing."

"God, Paula," Sophia groaned, massaging her scalp and doubling over in her seat. "Give me a break, will you?"

"Is this about me?" Paula punched her thumb between her ample bosom. "Am I in the doghouse because this is the first chance I've had to meet with you since you called last week about brainstorming what your investigators found?"

"No." Pursing her lips, Sophia reclined on the chair. "No, it's not that. I've been crazy busy and I *know* you have."

It was true. The D.A.'s office had been drowning in work, diligently trying to solidify their case against Waymon Cole following Judge Oswald's Stowe's unexpected overturn of the arraignment judge's decision to deny bail.

Sophia had been just as busy. She'd gotten the last of her things settled in her new office uptown and was learning about her new responsibilities. She'd made a point of assuring herself and others that she wouldn't be content riding a desk for the duration of her career. She planned to be just as active in the field.

If Sophia had learned one thing since her first full week as chief of detectives, it was that the position came with loads of paperwork. Just as well, since it looked like her personal life had returned to its normal state of grace. She hadn't spoken to Santigo since their "date" over a week ago. He hadn't called and she hadn't expected that he would. The ball was clearly in her court. Sophia had only to decide what to do with it.

Something nagged at her conscience—had been since Tigo's reappearance in her life. It was something that warned her not to misjudge him. Had she misjudged him? Had she allowed her fears—her suspicions resulting from the past—to wreak havoc on her ability to trust him in the present?

There was another booming sound, and Sophia realized that Paula had dropped another heavy book on the desk.

"Sorry, Pauly—"

"Stop." Paula barely lifted a hand. "Go handle your private life because I know all this has something to do with Tigo."

"No, it—"

"Hush." Paula linked her fingers and rested her chin atop them. "Get out of here and go see to your personal life while you're lucky enough to have one."

She was right. Sophia knew. "Thanks for understanding."

Paula tilted her head toward the door. "Get out of here. We'll talk about this mess later, and I'll see you tomorrow night."

Sophia only frowned.

"Jeez." Paula rolled her eyes. "Is it so bad that you've forgotten your own party?"

"Crap." Sophia slapped a palm to her forehead. "Veronica Hail, what have you done?"

"Aw, get over it. They're proud of you is all."

Sophia breathed out a snort that turned into soft laughter. "Yeah…yeah, I know they are. Thanks, Paula." She smiled when her friend simply waved her off like an annoying gnat.

Sophia walked through the city hall lobby on the way to her car—to Tigo to salvage whatever part of their renewed relationship was strong enough to weather their most recent storm. Her phone vibrated through the breast pocket of the three-quarter-length honey-wheat blazer she wore. She smiled, seeing her father's name on the faceplate.

"Hey, Daddy," she said, taking the tall revolving doors leading outside the hall.

"You sound good, baby girl. Lookin' forward to your party, huh?"

Sophia shook her head. "Let's just say that I've accepted the fact that your wife is an unbeatable opponent."

Gerald's rich, throaty laughter filtered through the phone's line. "I know that very well, which is why I have such a happy marriage."

"I don't even know what time to be there or where *there* is." Sophia felt her pockets for keys.

"Your mama said around six at the house so you can be there to greet the guests."

"Yippee." Sophia was less than jubilant but smiled for two female detectives who greeted her as she took the steps down from the building. "Daddy, thanks for calling to let me know."

"Well, um, that's not the only reason I called, baby."

Sophia's steps slowed as she noted the sudden loss of lightness from the man's voice. "Dad?"

"I need you to stop by my office before lunchtime tomorrow. I apologize, it being a Saturday and all. I know you probably have plans with Tigo—"

"Dad, what's wrong?" Her father was rambling. Gerald Hail *never* rambled.

"I have a friend in trouble."

"A friend? Daddy…"

"I swear it's a friend. He thinks his business is in trouble and that his kids are in the thick of the mess."

Sophia arrived at her reserved space outside the hall. "Who's the friend?" She disengaged the door locks and settled into the Charger.

"Sly Greenway."

Her hand faltered over the key in the ignition. "Sylvester Greenway of Greenway Construction."

"That's the one. Can you make time, baby?"

She was already nodding. "Of course I can, Daddy. Um…11:00 a.m. okay?"

"It's great. I'll let Sly know. And, baby? Thank you."

"No need for that, Daddy. I'll see you in the morning."

"Love you, baby."

"Love you, too, Daddy." Sophia smiled at the phone once the connection broke. She tossed it onto the passenger seat and started the car. She'd just angled out of the prime parking spot when she was thrown clear across the gear console. She hit the passenger side window with such force that everything went dark.

Outside the ruined car, a massive black pickup withdrew from the wreckage and made a speedy escape.

Chapter 12

Tigo was behind his desk, perched on the edge. His calf bumped the seat of the chair, moving it to and fro as he blandly observed the downtown view from his office window.

Puffing out his cheeks, he sent another withering look toward the invite he'd received by messenger a week earlier. A party for Sophia to celebrate her promotion. Would she want him there? he wondered. All he'd do is cast a shadow over it for her, anyway, since she figured he was as against her job as he'd always been.

And wasn't he? Silently, he posed the question to himself and gave the chair one firm bump that sent it twirling. What man in his right mind would be all right with the woman he treasured dealing with scum and putting her life on the line every day? Tigo admitted that he hadn't become that evolved yet.

But if acceptance of her career was the only way he could have her, then so be it. Now if only he could get *her* to believe that. He slapped the envelope on his knee. The party might be a good place to start, he thought. Then another thought struck him. Why wait for the party? Maybe he could take her if he had the chance to talk to her—explain…apologize.

With a decisive nod, he grabbed his phone and then made a fist when he discovered how badly his hand was shaking. When the office door suddenly flew open, he didn't know whether to curse or celebrate his assistant's arrival.

"Santigo, there you are! I looked for you in here just a few minutes ago." Jenny Boyce's fluster made her already high-pitched voice just under a scream. "What are you still doing here?"

"I've got that meeting with Carver and his people, remember?" Tigo smiled, then frowned a little after observing the woman closely. "They could only do this on a Saturday?" he asked when Jenny still appeared bewildered.

"You don't know." Jenny ceased her gaping as realization gradually crept into her wide brown eyes.

"What?" A bit of Tigo's teasing persona returned as his smile deepened. "Linus and Eli finally voted me out on my ass?"

"Tigo…" Jenny pushed a hand beneath her coarse dark hair where it rested at her shoulders and began to nervously massage her neck. "Honey, it—it's Sophia." She blinked, appearing to lose her nerve to say more. "Haven't you seen the news?" The words rushed out in a shaky sigh.

Santigo ignored the dull flutter of uneasiness in the pit of his stomach. "Tell me." He eased off the desk, exhibiting great calm that was totally fake.

Jenny clasped her hands. "There was a—an accident. Yesterday right around rush hour she—"

"Where is she?" Tigo had already rounded the desk and was gripping Jenny's shoulders; his fingertips bit into her ruffled pearl-colored blouse.

"They've got her at Mercy Hospital."

The strength left Tigo's legs, and he turned to grope for the edge of his desk. He would've surely missed the spot where he'd intended to sit were it not for Jenny's quick reflexes. She caught his arm and struggled with his weight while attempting to get him settled.

Linus and Eli arrived soon after, their handsome faces awash with concern. Eli went to Jenny and drew her into a reassuring squeeze while Linus saw to Tigo.

"Get him some water, Jen," Eli told the woman, mostly to give her something to do.

"She—she—is she…is she dead?" Tigo's breathing was so labored, he had a hand clutched at the center of the olive-green shirt he wore.

"No, man." Linus reached up to grab Tigo's face, forcing him to look into his eyes. "She's not. She's not, you hear me?" He gave Tigo's face a shake and then moved his hands down to his shoulders. "She just got banged up pretty bad in her car."

Elias took the water from Jenny and passed it to Tigo.

"Was it an accident?"

Eli slanted a quick look to Linus, and they both shook their heads in reply.

"We can't be sure, man," Eli said. "Witness accounts say a truck rammed the car and then drove off."

The glass slipped out of Tigo's hand and hit the carpeted floor with a muffled thud.

"Man, let's get you on the sofa," Linus urged, already drawing up his sleeves to assist his friend.

Tigo refused, simply extending a hand to ward off the contact. "I left her…I left her there the other night in that restaurant. I got pissed off…. Stupid!" he slammed a fist on his desk.

"Don't do that, T." Eli moved close. "This wasn't your fault."

"That's a lie." Tigo shook his head frantically, his chest

heaving uncontrollably. "What if they'd come after her that night?"

"Listen to me, T." Linus fisted Tigo's shirt and gave him a jerk. "Don't do that, either. Now, we don't even know all the facts. Regardless of what we suspect, this could've damn well been an accident."

"I need to see her." Tigo left the desk, and papers flew while he searched for his keys.

Linus got to them first, vaulting them over to Eli in an effortless move. "You can't drive right now, man. I'll take you."

Tigo looked ready to argue but saw that his friends were serious. He was certainly in no physical or mental state to take them both on, so he let it go.

"I, um… The meeting—"

Elias tossed the keys back to Linus. "Don't think about it now. I'll talk to Carver and the guys. Go see about your girl." He traded nods with Linus and watched him help Tigo out the door.

"I'm fine. I didn't even bump my head." Sophia presented her case from her hospital bed as she watched her mother moving around the room in a fit of nervous energy.

"They don't put fine people in the hospital." Veronica straightened the already straight bed linens. "Clearly something's wrong with you if you think you're *fine* after almost being crushed to death in your car."

Behind Veronica, Sophia saw her father shake his head in an attempt to warn her to let his wife have her say. Sophia, however, could see how terrified her mother was, and she only wanted to reassure her.

"Mama, I didn't even hit my head. It was my shoulder that hit the glass. My head hit the spot beneath the window and my shoulder only feels a little sore. Honestly, you're as bad as Paula." The fiery D.A. had been turning the hospital upside down since her arrival that morning. "There's nothing for you to be worried about."

"Thank you, Doctor," Veronica replied as she fluffed Sophia's pillows. "Why don't we ask a *real* M.D. what he thinks of your diagnosis?"

Dr. Bennett Freeman chuckled as he finished his notes in Sophia's chart. "I know she's getting on your nerves, Miss V."

"Hey!" Sophia called out in protest.

"But it really is good that she's so talkative and aware," Ben continued after sending Sophia a conspiratorial wink. "She's able to recall specifics from the accident and preliminary tests don't have us worried that there's been any serious or lasting damage." His light brown eyes narrowed. "That shoulder of hers may look a fright for a couple of weeks, but that's about it. She was very lucky."

"Prove it." Sophia clasped her hands to her chest. "Let me go home today."

"Nothin' doin'." A wave of seriousness washed over Ben's attractive tanned face.

Veronica folded her arms over her chest; her fair oval face beamed.

"I'm keeping you through the weekend," Ben went on. "Something tells me you won't adhere to strict bed rest if I release right now." He set the chart back in place at the foot of the bed. "Dinner should arrive shortly."

"Oh, Ben? What about her care after release?" Veronica followed the doctor from the room to discuss the matter.

Sophia pushed her head back into the pillows. "Gosh, Ben's gonna need a few days in a psych ward after that conversation."

Gerald chuckled, walking over to kiss his daughter's cheek. "If you didn't want to go to that party all you had to do was say so."

Father and daughter shared a laugh at Veronica's expense.

Then Sophia took note of the concern and fear in Gerald's charcoal-gray eyes, and she pulled him into a tight hug.

Gerald was wiping his eyes when he pulled away. "You better not tell your mother that I broke down."

Sophia laughed. "You have my word. Oh! Dad, the meeting with Mr. Greenway."

"Hush." Gerald grimaced. "That's the last thing you should be thinking about. I'll square it with Sly and we'll set up another meeting."

"I pray what happened to me won't scare him off."

"Why should it?"

Sophia bit her thumbnail and debated before she answered. "Daddy, you know Kenny and Ian were arrested for stealing a truck belonging to Greenway Construction. We believe they were unknowingly transporting something they shouldn't have been." She folded her arms across the hospital gown. "Is that what Mr. Greenway wants to talk about?"

"I don't think he knows." Gerald released an amazed sigh. "Given what he thinks his boys are tied up in, he might not be surprised by it, though."

"It'd be better if you didn't say anything." She squeezed her father's forearm when he massaged his jaw in a pensive fashion.

Gerald tweaked his daughter's nose. "Now you have *my* word," he said, hugging her again before he left to give Sophia time to rest.

Mercy Hospital was always in a state of uproar—from the emergency room to the intensive care unit, there was never a dull moment. That reality took on an entirely different outlook when D.A. Paula Starker arrived on the premises with her list of…suggestions.

"I'm sure you both agree that the new chief of detectives should be moved to a more secluded wing to be frequented only by her primary physician and the most essential staff."

Paula shifted her champagne-tinged stare between the two men she was conversing with. "I'm already making arrangements to assign security to her door. With the circuslike atmosphere around here, I'm sure you both understand."

Hospital Chief of Staff Chad Bavink and Chief of Police Dean Franklin studied the D.A. with impassive expressions.

"Circuslike?" Chief of Staff Bavink inhaled sharply.

"Forgive me, Chief." Paula smiled apologetically at the tall, solidly built man.

"Ms. Starker, don't you think we're getting ahead of ourselves here?" Chief Franklin huffed.

Paula looked as though she'd said nothing untoward. "Am I the only one who recalls that someone just tried to kill our new chief of Ds? Who, may I remind you, is currently finalizing a case on a very complex money-laundering scheme that's already taken down several employees of your organization?"

"We have no proof that one issue has anything to do with the other."

"And it's that kind of ignorance that has the force in the state it's in now."

"You're getting too full of yourself now, Miss D.A." Franklin looked down at Paula in a condescending fashion. "Could it be all that flashy press you've been getting?"

"All right, you two." Chief Bavink moved between the heated duo. "Chief Franklin, I have to agree with Ms. Starker on this."

Paula made no attempt not to gloat.

"Idle down, Madam D.A." Bavink pinned her with a stern look. "I don't approve of all the extra bodies on my corridors, either, unless they're my patients or staff. We'll have Chief Hail moved someplace more remote for the duration of her stay."

"Remote?" Paula crossed her arms over her chest. "And how does that help with her security?"

"I can have the guards make a few extra rounds to her wing, but my security staff is stretched thin enough as it is. I don't have the manpower to put someone on her door twenty-four hours even if it is just for the weekend." He smiled thinly.

"That's something you'll have to take up with the chief here, but you'll need to do it somewhere else. With the, uh, 'circuslike' atmosphere around here, I'm sure you understand."

"We know how to take care of our own, Ms. Starker," Franklin said once Chief Bavink had excused himself.

"Hmph." Paula's smile sharpened her classically lovely features. "And you do a fine job of it, too." She waved in the general direction of Sophia's hospital room.

The chief moved in closer to Paula. "You have a good one, Madam D.A."

"Conceited ox," Paula muttered as the man stalked off. She massaged the bridge of her nose in an attempt to summon calm until her eyes set on the man she really needed to see.

She kept her gaze locked on Rook Lourdess so as not to lose him in the packed corridor.

"Rook," she greeted him, slightly breathless by the time she caught up. Paula was so relieved to see the security specialist that it took her some time to realize that she'd interrupted the conversation with the man at his side.

"Paula." Rook's very deep-set and captivating stare harbored no trace of agitation over the interruption. He squeezed her elbow in a welcoming manner. "Glad you found me in all this."

Aside from Paula's slow nod, Rook got no other response. He smiled, taking note of her fixed expression as she stared at one of his oldest friends. Putting a hand to her waist, he took the liberty of making introductions.

"Linus Brooks, Paula Starker."

It was a rare thing to find the sharp lawyer caught off balance. Paula didn't think she'd have believed it herself had someone tried to tell her. Eventually she accepted Linus's outstretched hand.

"Nice to meet you, too," she returned his greeting and then blinked as if to force a return of her senses. "Rook, um, thanks so much for coming over. Is this a good time to talk?" She looked at Linus again quickly.

Rook spread his hands. "It's what I'm here for." He sent Linus a sly wink and walked on past to take the beautiful D.A. with him.

Linus didn't notice Rook's gesture; his attention was being held captive by the woman at his side.

Gerald Hail had left his daughter's hospital room some fifteen minutes earlier to find his wife, who was most likely still talking to Dr. Freeman. Sophia took advantage of the solitude to catch a nap. The soft drone of the headline news channel and the muted sounds of mixed conversation outside the room door made for an effective lullaby.

Tigo was more conscious of his movements when he entered the room to find her asleep. He took great care to keep his footfalls silent as he moved toward the bed. Once he was there, he merely stared, memorizing every curve of her face. Tentatively he reached out to smooth the back of his hand across the soft line of her jaw. The bottomless well of his stare appraised the flawless mahogany-brown of her skin and the curl of her hair.

The shuddering sigh he expelled was enough to rouse Sophia from her snooze. She blinked several times in rapid succession at the sight of him standing over her.

"Tig?"

He raised his head suddenly at the sound of her voice. "Hey." His tone was light, unsteady. A furrow settled between the heavy sleekness of his brows as he fought to rein in his emotions.

He reached out to fuss with her hair again and expelled a

halfhearted laugh. "You know, you didn't have to do all *this* to get out of goin' to your mom's party."

Her resulting laughter was soft, but it was there. A wave of sobriety overwhelmed them suddenly and Sophia studied Tigo's fist burrowed into the covers. Uncertainly at first, she stroked the back of his hand.

"Thanks for what you did for the guys. Mama told me you got them new lawyers." She kept her gray stare on her fingers trailing his hand. "Why didn't you tell me you were helping them?"

"Never came up." He sat on the edge of the bed. "Kenny and Ian…their dads work for Joss." He raised his chin in a brief up-and-down move. "How'd *you* get involved?"

"My parents." Sophia tugged at the cuff of his shirt and then smoothed her fingers across the fine stitching there. "They've been friends with the Bradfords for years. They asked me to help out." She laughed again with a bit more strength than before. "I thought it'd be a relatively simple assignment. One that'd keep me out of trouble but…guess I'm just a trouble magnet."

Her words, spoken in jest, broke what resolve Tigo was fighting to uphold. When he bowed his head then, Sophia could tell that his shoulders were shaking.

"Tig, don't…shh…" Gingerly, she eased up to pull him down into her embrace. They held the awkward position for long moments. She raked her nails across the soft dark waves tapering at his neck.

"I'm fine. Please believe that." She feathered lazy kisses across his forehead and temple. "I just got knocked around a little bit."

Tigo sniffled, then growled out a curse over his loss of control. "I'm sorry, Sophie. I shouldn't have left you like that—in the restaurant—"

"It's okay—"

"Don't do that." Muscles danced along his jaw as he looked

at her stonily. "Don't forgive me for that. They could've come after you—"

"Tig, listen to me." She firmed her hold on his unyielding biceps. "This is no one's fault but the creep who smashed my car, damn it." It was her turn to growl then. "I really loved that car."

Tigo shuddered again, rubbing at the pressure of unspilled tears behind his eyes.

She pulled the hand to her chest and squeezed. "I'm so sorry you heard about this."

"Why?" The whisper held an edge.

Sophia kept her eyes down. "It's just one more black mark beside my career, isn't it?"

His hand tightened on hers. "You're crazy if you think I wouldn't want to know about this."

"Tig—"

"Stop." He leaned close to bring his face level with hers. "I know how bullheaded I was the other night, and I know how bullheaded I was to give that ultimatum back when you first started on the force. I'm sorry for that, Soap, but sooner or later you're gonna have to let it go and accept what I'm telling you right now."

He began to shake his head. "I'm not goin' anywhere, Soap. To get rid of me, you'll have to arrest me and find some way to keep me locked up." He smiled when she laughed, then quickly returned to being serious. "Honey, we'll never have a damn thing until you believe that." He kissed her forehead, the tip of her nose. "Get some rest."

"You're going?" Her hand tightened on his.

"Remember what I said." He cupped her cheek. "I'm not going anywhere, but you need to get some rest." He turned his head to look the bed over. "If I stay I'll want to get in there with you."

"I wouldn't mind that." Her tone was as eager as her expression.

"Trust me, if I wind up in there, rest will be nonexistent."
He crushed her mouth beneath his.

Sophia emitted needy moans while thrusting her tongue
desperately against his. "Please stay."

He withdrew with an exaggerated sigh. "Close your eyes."
He began to tuck the sheets in around her.

Sophia was too worn-out to argue and did as she was told.
She was asleep within minutes.

Chapter 13

Monday morning found Sophia slipping into her favorite old pair of sneakers. She hesitated while tying the second pair of laces and took time to thank God for her life and for letting Tigo be part of it again. Then she asked Got to please help her to not mess it up again. She finished tying her laces and knew that request was easy to ask for.

Somehow she had to work on her trust skills. Trust was easy to give and take, yet it was hard to maintain. The hazards of being a cop, she acknowledged with half a shrug.

"Figure it out later, Sophia." Just then, she was ready to sign her release papers, take her wheelchair ride and get the hell out of there.

"Are you sure it wouldn't be better to keep her for another few days?"

Sophia's excitement began to wane when her parents walked in with Dr. Freeman.

"I don't see any reason for it."

Sophia let out a small sigh of relief at Ben's response to her mother.

"It'll still be another few days before I clear her for active duty," he continued. "But there's no reason to tie her down here."

"Thank you." Sophia sent her parents a happy wave of triumph.

"Oh, honey, you're dressed." Veronica seemed rather perturbed by the fact. "I could've helped."

"I could handle it, but a hug would be nice."

The Hails melted over their daughter's request and were all too happy to oblige.

Ben smiled, sending a quick wink at his patient before he made a quiet exit. Gerald kissed his daughter's forehead and then his wife's cheek before he moved to the far side of the room to give the women a measure of privacy.

"I'm sorry, baby, for acting like a mother hen." Tears suddenly sparkled in Veronica's light eyes. "I um…" She fussed with Sophia's hair, pulling it from the collar of her sweatshirt. "I used to hate it when your grandma Este did that." She referred to her mother, Estelle Reed.

"It's all right, Mama." Sophia squeezed her hand. "It's only because you care."

Veronica nodded and sniffled lightly. "I care and I love you, but that's not all of it." She looked back at her husband, taking comfort in his nod. "So much of it has to do with Viva."

Sophia felt her heart lurch at the sound of her sister's name.

Veronica brushed away tears and sniffled again. She pressed kisses on the backs of Sophia's hands.

"Your daddy and me wouldn't survive if we lost you, too."

"Mama…" Sophia's voice was hushed. "Mama, that won't happen."

Veronica's smile was sad with knowing. "That's what your sister said when she went off to California."

Sophia bowed her head and decided not to remind her mother that not accepting Viva's profession had a lot to do with her choice to head out West.

"I know most of the blame lies right at our feet." Veronica seemed to be reading her daughter's mind then. "We just don't want to make the same mistake twice."

When Veronica sniffled again, Sophia pulled the woman close. Mother and daughter were still embracing when the doctor returned.

"We ready?" Ben asked.

Still holding on to her mother, Sophia smiled. "Ready."

The ball was once again in her court, Sophia thought as she checked her phone messages later that day to discover that Santigo hadn't called. She knew he was waiting for her to rise to the challenge he'd laid down during their conversation when he'd visited on Saturday.

Their time together on Sunday had been brief but sweet. Conversation had steered clear of anything serious. They watched a few pregame sports shows while enjoying the nonhospital breakfast he'd smuggled in. He was gone before lunch, and Sophia hadn't heard from him since.

The doorbell broke into her thoughts, and Sophia tossed the phone on the living room sofa en route to answer. Hoping to find Tigo in the hall, she opened the door without hesitation. It was Paula, and Sophia's disappointment couldn't have been more evident.

"Don't worry about thanking me for the sexy security detail outside your door." Paula rolled her eyes and brushed past Sophia on her way inside. "But a smile of welcome is just good manners, you know?" She tossed her hooded sweater on an armchair.

"I was hoping to see Tig." Sophia pushed her door shut and then leaned back against it.

"So you haven't seen him since he came to see you yesterday morning," Paula said matter-of-factly while heading for the kitchen.

"How did—?" Sophia threw up a hand when the answer hit her. "So my security detail is here to report on my social life, too. Hmph, funny, I thought that's what my style team was for."

"Oh, get over it." Paula's voice rose from the refrigerator, where her head was buried. "After what happened we aren't taking any chances. Have you heard from any of your siblings in blue?"

Sophia ambled into the kitchen, her worn hot-pink house shoes slapping on the hardwood floor. "I'll be having a breakfast meeting with Roy Poltice and some of the other brass." She watched Paula pour two glasses of apple juice.

"Don't try shirking the guards I've got on you, So-So," Paula warned. "They're gorgeous, but they're brainy and are damn good at what they do."

"Don't be shy." Sophia accepted the juice. "Tell me what you *really* think." Gray eyes narrowed, she leaned across the table to consider Paula. "You think some of the top brass are involved in this, don't you?"

"And you're a fool if you don't. Judge Stowe is dirty and he's an idiot." Paula took a long gulp of the juice. "He's gotten away with being dirty for a long time. That doesn't happen unless you've got friends way up the food chain. Now—" she drained the glass and set it aside to go rifle through the kitchen cabinets "—what have you got to eat in here?"

"What's this about?" Linus asked Tigo when he arrived in the smaller conference room at Joss Construction.

"Got a call from Ian's and Ken's lawyers last night." Tigo didn't turn from the beverage cart, where he added cream to his coffee. "They want to thank me and do some explaining." His rust-colored shirt bunched at the shoulder when he shrugged.

"'Kay…that's…nice—why do *we* have to be here?" Linus asked as Elias entered the room.

"Attorneys say Ian mentioned there was something we needed to know." Tigo sighed, turning from the cart with a tall mug in hand. "Said we needed to keep our eyes open."

The three partners were still frowning over the cryptic advisement when a buzzer sounded from a box on the center of the round table in the room.

"Boys are here."

"Thanks, Des," Eli called out to his assistant.

Eli, Linus and Tigo took their spots around the table and waited. Shortly, Ian Roche and Kenny Bradford stepped into the room with their lawyers. The younger men made their rounds, shaking hands and nodding solemnly.

"You guys know there's a dedicated cop who's been working for you, too?" Tigo asked when the boys thanked him especially for all he'd done.

Kenny Bradford nodded eagerly, large brown eyes ablaze with acknowledgment. "Yes, sir. We already talked to Chief Hail."

"And she's okay with us having this little conversation?" Linus asked.

Ian nodded. "She understands why we needed to talk to you."

"Have a seat, guys." Eli waved a hand.

"We didn't steal that truck," Kenny blurted as though he were bursting at the seams to share. "Ian and me, we've been workin' to help our folks as much as possible with all the college expenses. That's why I took the job at Greenway and things were goin' real good." He smoothed damp palms across his black trousers. "The money was good but I wanted to make as much as I could so…" One hand fisted. "When the guys hooked me up with the cop, I was interested."

"What cop?" Tigo asked.

"Rick Jessup. I—I think he's new. Anyway, he told me

Greenway needed somebody to drive trucks for overtime. I went on about three or four runs before I even thought about bringing Ian into it." Kenny looked over at his friend.

"Did anybody have problems with Ian being involved?" Eli asked.

"Didn't seem like it." Kenny rolled his bottom lip between his teeth and shook his head. "They wanted to hire Ian on the regular, but they knew he already had the job here with Joss with his dad being one of the top crew chiefs, like mine."

Tigo's midnight gaze slanted toward his partners, then to the lawyers. Both men nodded to confirm Tigo's unspoken suspicion.

"The cop who approached Kenny had a crisis of conscience," Dale Eagers explained. "According to him, the guys were set up to take the fall if and when they ever got caught up in some mess. Kenny and Ian didn't know they were transporting cash, so when they were stopped, whoever's pulling the strings at Greenway could easily deny they had knowledge. Their ties to Joss pinned them as expendable."

Linus's nasty curse was muttered too low for anyone to hear. "Always knew them fools were shady," he said a bit louder.

The boys' other lawyer, Hilda Graves, nodded her agreement. "The folks at Greenway knew how easy it'd be for the guys' dads to get suspicious of all those after-hours trips all over town to areas where no construction projects were in progress or would be in progress."

"Sorry for all the trouble we caused." Ian's handsome honey-toned face was drooped and dour-looking.

Tigo reached over to pat the boy's arm left bare by his short sleeve. "You're good kids. Don't let anybody tell you different."

"Second that," Elias and Linus spoke simultaneously.

Some of the tension broke as the room warmed with laughter.

"You and your staff might want to investigate a possible link between Greenway, Waymon Cole and his laundering scheme," Tigo suggested to the attorneys and smirked ill-humoredly. "Money's got to be transported to be laundered, right?"

Hilda nodded and crossed her legs beneath a pair of cream-colored slacks. "Thanks to Chief Hail, we're on it. We're petitioning the judge to have all charges against our clients dropped."

"Hopefully the *new* judge will be interested in hearing that motion."

"That's just what Chief Hail said," Dale Eagers shared before he winked and pushed back from the table. "If you all will excuse us, we've got a lot of work to do."

The partners remained quiet as the attorneys and their clients left the conference room.

"Chief Hail knows her stuff," Linus commented once he was alone with his colleagues.

"Damn right she does." Eli was next to rise from the table. "A man would be a fool to let a woman like that get away from him."

Tigo smiled but offered no comment.

"I'd say he'd be the biggest fool ever," Linus added. "You know, his friends would have to remind him of that for the rest of his life."

"It'd be their duty as friends to do just that."

"All right, all right." Tigo raised his hands at Eli's final barb. "I got it, I promise." Some of the humor left his face. "I swear I've done everything I can to convince her to give me another chance. Now it's up to her to believe I'm for real." He studied the table without really seeing it. "All I can do now is wait."

Later that day, Sophia shook hands with Sylvester Greenway, owner of Greenway Construction. They'd arranged to meet for a late lunch in the office her father kept at his textile facility just outside Philadelphia.

"My God, Ger, she's a beauty." The construction entrepreneur shook his head as though he was in a state of wonderment. The wonder soon morphed into concern. "How are you, love? I was so sorry to hear about the accident."

"Thank you, Mr. Greenway. I'm much better." Sophia tugged the cuffs of her gold wrap shirt and got comfortable in her seat. "Daddy tells me you want to talk about your business. What's the problem exactly?" She could see the unease clouding Sylvester Greenway's small dark eyes.

The man's simple reaction sent caution flaring in Sophia's gray eyes. "Mr. Greenway, you know—"

"I know what it means to talk to you, dear." Greenway sighed and dug his fingertips into the table. "Desperate measures are needed now. I've given my boys more than enough time to straighten up. They haven't."

At her nod, Gerald Hail rubbed his hands together. "Let's get some of those sandwiches in our stomachs while we talk. The cafeteria spent too much time on them for us not to enjoy."

"What's the problem, Mr. Greenway?" Sophia queried while everyone added condiments to their roast beef and chicken sandwiches.

"My boys are very ambitious." Greenway halted his movements. "I suppose I'm to blame for a lot of it. My company's always been in competition with Joss so…the boys often saw me coming home aggravated over some project Evan Joss had stolen out from under me." Greenway smirked while his thoughts settled on the founder of Joss Construction.

"At least I *thought* the guy had stolen the projects out from under me."

Sophia sliced her sandwich and smiled. "I understand, sir."

"Anyway…the guys always wanted the company to be the

biggest and best on the block." Sylvester accepted the glass of ginger ale Gerald Haii passed him.

"I did a good job teaching my sons how to be ambitious but not so much time teaching them how to be ethical." He sipped from the glass and appeared to be in deep thought.

"I don't think it bothered me much until I noticed all the cops hanging around the building."

Slowly Sophia returned her sandwich to its plate.

"The guys told me they'd added protection for the business, but the cops didn't seem too interested in protection, only the packages they collected the one day they were there during the week." He waved a hand. "They were always there on different days, too." He pushed back his plate.

"I knew then that my boys were in bed with dirty cops. I didn't even have to ask. I don't know why I reported that truck stolen. Desperate to disturb the roaches, I guess…not sure why I thought the truck had anything to do with those cops."

"Good instincts." Gerald commended his old friend.

Greenway shrugged. "The boys don't think I notice much of what's going on." He chuckled. "Maybe I just wanted to get their attention."

Gerald leaned toward his friend. "You sure you're ready to pin somethin' like this on your own kids? Put 'em in a bind with the law?"

No remorse kindled in the man's small yet brilliant stare. "My kids are already in a bind with the law." He looked at Sophia. "This is the only way I know to get them out of it."

Sophia was dead tired when she returned home that evening. She'd planned to stop by to talk with Santigo following the late lunch with her father and Sylvester Greenway, but she was too beat to head anywhere but back home. She chalked it up to still recovering from the accident and promised herself that they'd hash it out soon.

Closing the door at her back, Sophia leaned there, taking in long refreshing breaths in hopes of calming her mind. She reached beneath her blazer, intending to unholster her weapon, when a sound from the kitchen caught her ear.

Immediately alert, she drew and aimed her weapon as she covered the living room on silent steps.

"What in the hell?" She let the weapon fall to her side as she sank back in renewed relief on the door frame.

Viva Hail was a chirpy, younger replica of her mother, Veronica. "You still take cream in your coffee, Soapy?" She turned when her sister remained silent, smiled and spread her arms for a hug.

Sophia didn't hesitate. She closed the distance to draw her sister into a fierce embrace. "How'd you get in here?" Her words were muffled in the coils of thick light brown curls that bounced over Viva's head.

"Rook's guys are always such suckers for women in distress." Viva sighed.

"Woman in distress." Sophia pulled back to give her sister the once-over. "Or maybe they just know to give the love of their boss's life anything she wants."

"That's not me anymore." Viva pushed Sophia's hair from her face.

Sophia reciprocated the move with Viva's hair. "Whatever," she returned.

The sisters hugged again.

"How are you?" Viva asked.

"Much better now." Sophia smiled, not realizing how much she had missed her big sister until she was in her arms.

Viva allowed anxiety to flood her movie-star lovely features. "What have you gotten yourself into? Dirty cops, Soapy?" she gently scolded.

"And I'm *this* close to getting to the bottom of it." Sophia positioned her index finger and thumb inches apart.

"Why? Because they're trying to kill you?" Viva eased

both hands into the back pockets of her jeans and grimaced. "I suppose this is funny to you?" She watched Sophia look smug.

The smugness didn't last long. "Why are we talking about this?" Sophia removed her denim blazer and the black leather holster, replacing her service weapon inside. "What I want to know is what you're doing in town. How'd you find out about the accident in the first place?"

"It's the technological age, Miss Ol' School." Viva patted her sister's cheek. "But I actually owe it to Murray. He keeps an eye on everything that happens back here." Viva went back to the counter, where she'd been preparing the coffee. "When he told me, I was on the first plane."

Sophia accepted the mug of coffee her sister offered and conjured up the image of Viva's bodyguard turned agent Murray Dean.

"Jeez." Sophia frowned into the deep mug. "You never add enough sugar." She went to the counter to remedy the issue. "Seen Mama and Daddy yet? Somebody's gotta be the bigger person, V," she added when silence met her question.

Viva bowed her head, studying the contents of her own mug. "I know."

"And I know they regret where things stand." Sophia sipped the sweeter coffee and smiled at the taste. "They know it wasn't your fault."

Viva's full, naturally pouty lips parted in disbelief. "Are you tryin' to tell me that the great Veronica Hail admitted she was wrong?"

"Why don't you call her and find out?"

Viva twisted her mouth as if she was contemplating. "Too much to think about on an empty stomach." She shook her head.

"Well, don't look to my kitchen for sustenance." Sophia pulled the tails of her coral-colored blouse from her slacks.

"Don't I know it? And I already ordered pizza. Should be

here by the time you slip into something suitable for a girl's night in." Viva winked saucily.

"On it!" Sophia was already halfway out of the kitchen when she turned and went back to her sister for another hug.

Forty-five minutes later, Sophia and Viva were in the throes of girlish giggles and indulging in an extra-large veggie and three-cheese pizza. They took time to catch their breaths and drank deeply to quench their thirsts. Wine for Viva. Beer for Sophia.

"So I guess you're still livin' the single life." Viva studied the light filtering through her glass of chardonnay. "I didn't notice any, uh…male paraphernalia in your bathroom, unless you count the condoms in your medicine cabinet."

Sophia's cheeks puffed as she struggled to swallow the beer she'd just chugged. "Still haven't mastered the art of the segue," she said once her verbal skills had returned.

Viva shrugged. "I thought I did good to wait *that* long." She took another sip of wine and relished the flavor. "So who is he? Or do I even need to ask?"

Sophia's expression had Viva tilting her head back to expel the laughter that flooded her throat.

"I wondered how long you'd be able to deny yourself that man! So how long's it been going on? You know I want all the details."

"Hmph." Sophia downed more of her beer. "The *details* are all wrapped up in my job."

"Ouch." Viva recalled too well how little the cop life mixed with Santigo Rodriguez.

"He really seems to be trying though, Veev."

"So he's had a change of heart?"

"Not exactly." Sophia lay flat on the sofa, balancing the beer bottle on her stomach. "He still despises the job but says he doesn't care so long as we're together."

"Sounds fantastic." Viva sat her glass on the coffee table

and reached for the bowl of chips there. "So why do you look so down about it?"

"I wasn't… At first I was…stressing over the fact that maybe Tig wasn't being honest with himself, that sooner or later he'd admit we were a mistake."

"But he's not doing that." Viva smoothed a hand over the sleeve of her teal-green sweater.

Sophia pressed the cool bottom of the beer bottle on her forehead. "Looks like he's for real."

"You believe him?"

"I was on my way to tell him so when my car got smashed all to hell."

"But you've seen him since then? So what's stopping you now?"

Sophia pushed up to lean on her elbow. "I think he wants me to think about it."

"Have you?"

"Till my brain hurts."

Viva shifted her weight on the armchair she'd claimed. "So I guess you should pay a visit to your man before you dot the precinct's door in the morning, huh?"

Sophia tilted her beer bottle in a mock toast. "Just what I was thinking."

Chapter 14

Unfortunately for Sophia, the precinct did come calling for her before she could get to more enjoyable matters that morning. Fortunately, the breakfast meeting with the top brass didn't last very long.

Sophia hadn't seen anything to relay clues about the accident, including the truck that supposedly hit her. She'd been fully cleared by her doctor, so that was no longer an issue, and she'd already decided to keep a lid on the unfolding details of the case. That play was due in part to the fact that she was still trying to put all the pieces together and partly because she didn't know who the hell to trust.

She hadn't realized how long it'd been since she'd visited Joss Construction until she was in the downtown high-rise that housed its headquarters. She located the executive wing and Tigo's office with relative ease. There was no trace of a receptionist or assistant when she arrived so, with tentative steps, she moved toward the door with Tigo's name engraved in the teakwood plate.

Sophia found him inside the office perched on the edge of his desk. He sat there, head bowed while he focused on the contents of a folder lying open on the surface of the desk.

She studied him contentedly, happy to spend the time at such a worthwhile task. She waited for him to close the folder before she cleared her throat and waved when he looked toward the door.

Gold flecks sparkled in his dark eyes; he blinked, the beginnings of a smile tugging at his mouth.

"Hey." His voice was deep, surprised. Slowly he pushed off his desk. "You all right?"

She gave him a quick nod. "I was just um…hoping…"

His smile deepened and his eyes faltered to her chest, which heaved with unconscious allure beneath the black silk of her blouse. "It's good to hope." His eyes returned to her face. "Would you mind sharing?"

"I was just hoping that I waited long enough to bring our conversation back to where it was last Saturday." She crossed the office threshold.

"I don't want to rush you." He seemed to sober. "Not about this, not this time."

She shook her head; curls dangling from her updo bounced at her neck. "It's no rush, and you deserve a response."

Tigo nodded as though approving her decision. He returned to the desk, where he leaned against the polished walnut and hid his hand in one pocket of his midnight-blue trousers.

Sophia mimicked Tigo's stance after she'd closed the office door and leaned back against it. "I told you I'd been waiting on the other shoe to drop since we started seeing each other again. I'm sorry but…I didn't expect us to last past the first few nights." She shrugged one slender shoulder. "I wanted to enjoy as much of us as I could and close myself off to the serious stuff."

Tigo watched his shoe for a time. "The serious stuff." The

heel of a black wingtip bumped the bottom of the desk. "Like whether or not you love me?"

"I love you." She did not hesitate to assure him. "I've always loved you and I never stopped, but, Tig…those feelings didn't stop us from fizzling out before, did they?"

"Sophia, we were kids. *I* was an idiot," he rasped, then smiled at the sound of her laughter.

She soon sobered. "We weren't all that young and you weren't that much of an idiot. See, sooner or later my job would've become a problem for us—one we couldn't have fought. You know it's true." She watched a muscle flex at his jawbone.

"And what about now?" He focused on rubbing his hands one inside the other. "Your job is still an issue we can't fight, and I need you to understand this, Sophie." He looked at her. "I'm done fighting. I'm already at acceptance if that's what it takes to have you."

"That day I had the accident…I was leaving city hall to come tell you that it didn't matter, that I wanted you for however long we'd have and that I didn't care where the shoe dropped or *if* it dropped."

Tigo left the desk and came to gather her in his arms. They embraced desperately.

"I'm sorry." He buried a kiss in her neck.

She locked her arms around his. "So am I. But, Tig, I'm scared—I don't know how I'd get through losing you again."

He stepped back to cup her face in his wide palms. "We just have to make sure it doesn't happen again, then."

The kiss had starving intensity when their lips melded. Sophia felt her heart flipping as Santigo massaged the small of her back before sliding his hands across her butt. He cupped the cheeks filling out the pin-striped slacks she sported.

Exercising very little silence, Tigo set her against the door. Sophia cried out, which allowed his tongue the room it needed for a thorough exploration of her mouth.

"You're gonna get yourself in trouble." Her lashes fluttered as his fingers handled her with wicked expertise.

"Are you serious?" His chuckle was humor and sensuality entwined. "Do you know how many times Eli's had Clarissa up in here? And don't get me started on Linus and his…friends."

"Are you trying to tell me you've been a good boy?"

"I've been an angel."

Sophia felt the door's cool wood against her skin and discovered that he'd relieved her of her blouse and was already lowering the straps of her camisole. He'd set her gun holster on the table nearest the door.

"How'd you learn to do that so smoothly?"

"An angel never tells," he growled into her neck. And then he was unhooking her bra and drawing it from her shoulders.

"Tigo, wait. I can't." Though insanely aroused, she thought one of them should exercise a cool head. Difficult since he'd set her higher against the door to suckle her nipples.

"If that's the case," he said even as his mouth worked over her, "we're gonna have problems. No way am I letting you out of here like this."

"You could give me my clothes."

"I can give you more than that." He took her from the door and charted a direct path to the sofa.

"Be serious, Tig." Her words carried on a moan. "Anyone could walk in…."

"Hmm…" Sudden consideration crossed his gorgeous face along with an unmistakable lacing of humor. "You're right." He went back to the door, locked it and continued their journey to the long sofa set catty-corner from his desk.

"Any more precautions I should take?" he asked once she was on her back and half-naked beneath him.

"Well, you being an angel and all." Her captivating dark eyes harbored a devilish gleam. "Don't suppose you keep a stash of condoms lying around?"

"Hell." Bested by the remark, Tigo's unfairly long lashes settled down to shield his stare. Then he gave a quick shake of his head and expertly unfastened her trousers. "Guess I'll have to improvise."

Sophia didn't begrudge the fit of hysterical giggles she gave in to then. She was too happy. She felt pliant, free, utterly relaxed. Tigo used that to his advantage. He jerked her out of what remained of her clothing.

Her laughter ended on a high gasp when he kissed the dip of her thigh, mere centimeters from her sex. There, his tongue bathed her languidly until her fingers grew tight in his hair. She tugged, silently urging him to take her with his mouth.

"Will you make me beg, Tig?"

He obliged instead, thrusting his tongue deep, slowly rotating as her hips circled.

Settling himself comfortably at the juncture of her thighs, Tigo held one of her shapely legs across the back of the sofa. He kept her other thigh flat, providing him ample space for his erotic endeavor. Immobile, Sophia dragged her fingers through her hair and expelled a shaky moan while Tigo growled his approval.

Somewhere, a phone rang, but it was ignored. Sophia was so thoroughly starved for Santigo's touch that his intimate inspection of her body brought her to climax much sooner than she'd expected…or wanted…

The pressure of release built at an amazing rate. Her thighs trembled so that Tigo tightened his hold on both limbs and went about ravishing her with increasing depth and determination.

The sound of the ringing phone resumed—again it went unchecked. Sophia tugged one of the gold throw pillows across her face in hopes of smothering her progressively breathy cries. A flood of moisture gushed then, bathing Santigo's tongue as he nourished himself with her essence.

* * *

Later, the rich, rhythmic sounds of their breathing filled the room. Sophia was first to recover, wriggling her bare form beneath Tigo's clothed one.

"I hope I haven't ruined your sofa." She suckled his earlobe.

He lifted his head, those uncommon gold flecks glistening in the inky black of his stare. "I can replace everything in here except you."

Their kiss was a sweet peck that ended with the buzzing of the phone moments later. "I think that's you," he said against her mouth.

"It can wait." She wrinkled her nose toward the direction she thought the phone may've been. Then she studied him keenly. "I haven't taken care of you." She smoothed her lips across the angle of his jaw.

"I'm fine," he muttered into her neck as he nuzzled his face there.

When he lifted his head, Sophia's tongue darted out to retrace his jaw.

"You'll definitely be making it up to me, Chief." He nudged up her chin with his fist.

"Will you call me Chief while I'm making it up to you?" She bit down on her lip.

"Only if you promise to harass me."

"Oh, yes…in every way I can think of." She puckered her lips for the kiss he was already leaning in to give.

"Up we go." He relieved her of his weight, locking his hands on her wrists to pull her to sit.

Sophia battled a fit of reluctance and then inched herself off the sofa while Tigo made himself more comfortable on the chair. Happily, he ogled her while she tiptoed around the office collecting her clothes. She was buttoning her shirt over her underthings when the phone rang again.

"Guess our interlude's over." Tigo pushed off the sofa.

Sophia admired his unhurried stride as he returned to his desk. Sighing, she went to retrieve the phone from the floor, where it had fallen while Tigo took her out of her clothes.

She smiled at the sight of Detective Jofi Eames's name on the screen. "Don't tell me the precinct's falling apart since I left?" she teased. "Jofi?" she called when he didn't respond straight away.

"Sophie." The man's voice was scarcely a whisper.

"What?"

Her hushed tone caught Tigo's ear, and all his attention flowed toward her then. He moved from behind the desk when he saw her raise a trembling hand to her mouth.

"I know." She nodded, eyes closed. "Yeah, yeah, I understand." Blindly, she shoved the phone into her pocket.

Tigo didn't ask for details, only pulled her to him. Sophia did not resist.

It was nothing unusual to see a hoard of police cruisers at the department's garage, but the reason was usually for maintenance or repair. Never had they been called for a backup request.

Sophia entered the crime scene, or war zone as it were. She appeared as if she were walking through her own bad dream. The crime scene unit was already on the job, collecting evidence of the most miniscule proportions. Some dusted for fingerprints, of which there were tons; others took pictures. Though she had visited scores of scenes in the past, nothing could have prepared her for the image of her dear friend Harold Mackey lying in the blood that had left his body through an array of bullet wounds. Her boots felt glued to the floor as she knelt to study the P.D.'s chief mechanic lying prone on the cold, oil-splattered cement floor.

Hands on her shoulders made her jump, and she looked up at Jofi.

"Sorry, hon." He raised his hands defensively. "How are you?"

Sophia's weary laugh was answer enough.

"Come here." Jofi offered her refuge in a comforting hug.

Sophia pulled back. "I want details, Jof. Who was first on the scene? How'd this go down? Are there any suspects?"

Jofi bristled and took a quick glimpse of his shoes. "'Fraid you're lookin' at him, Soph. I was the shooter."

Her gray eyes widened to moons in shadow. The expression spoke volumes, and Jofi paced in a small circle as he relayed the afternoon's events.

"I got a call at the precinct—they wanted the captain and refused to talk to anybody but him. They got real nasty with the switchboard, so they patched the call through to me." Jofi tried to work out the bunched muscles in his neck. "Guy's voice sounded sort of familiar but I couldn't place it—he just told me to get to the garage."

Sophia squeezed her eyes shut and put more distance between herself and Harold's body.

"The place was empty when I got here. Empty…except for Harold. I must've interrupted him." Jofi shook his head as though to clear it. "He had an overnight bag, and I tried to ask him about the call. He got…got weird and then I could tell something was wrong. I thought maybe he had someone here in the shop. Maybe somebody was givin' him a hard time."

Jofi pulled his hands from his pockets and folded his arms over his chest. "I tried to get him to tell me what was up— subtly so we wouldn't tip off whoever was in here. Then things went from weirder to worse. He pulled his weapon when I moved to him. We went back and forth. I panicked— stupid! But it was Harold!" Jofi pressed his hands on the sides of his head. "Then he fired. Jesus… He missed. I fired—just to scare him, make him drop his weapon. I missed on purpose. He fired again and again and I—I knew he meant it. I had to take him down." Jofi's eyes were red when he looked at her. "God, Sophie, I'm sorry. I know how close—"

"What about the bag?" Sophia had turned to take a slower, closer observation of the scene. "You said Harold was carrying an overnight bag."

"Money." Jofi's expression hardened. "The bag was full of money."

Sophia closed her eyes. "Harold," she whispered.

Late evening found Sophia in her office, doing her part in the damage control required following the day's events. She put the phone down, feeling like a broken record after issuing the canned statement her staff had prepared for the media.

Harold Mackey's death wasn't the only headline of the day. One of the city's impound supervisors, Ernest Lyman, had been found dead in his home in south Philly. The media so far had only put together that it was two deaths featuring city employees, but Sophia knew there was more. Ernest had been murdered. Someone had spooked Harold and called the station to sic the police on him. But who? One thing was sure: the decision had come from very high up the chain.

A single knock upon the tall, old-fashioned maple doors caused Sophia's teeth to ache. She couldn't take another upset that day. She was sure to dissolve into a screaming fit if she did. Finding Santigo leaning against the door frame brought a quick, easy smile to her mouth.

"Can I be of service to the chief of Ds?"

"I don't know," she said slowly, twirling her chair back and forth. "I'm in need of *lots* of service."

Leaving the door, Tigo strolled behind her desk and sat on the edge. Sophia scooted her chair close and rested her head on his knee.

"It'll be all right, Soap." He massaged her scalp and nape. "I'm sorry about Harold."

"They think he was dirty." She closed her eyes and inhaled the spicy, alluring scent of his cologne. "I can't let them ruin his name like that. He was a good man—a good cop."

"How do you plan to prove that?" He dragged his fingers up through her loose curls and then resumed the massage.

She turned her face into his thigh and groaned into the unyielding muscular expanse. "The answer's in my head somewhere, but my brain's too mushy to find it."

"Hey." Tigo pulled her up, drawing her between his thighs. "You need sleep. Let me take you home."

"Viva's there."

"Well, that's good." He ran his hands along her arms. "She'll make sure you get some rest."

She gave one singular, stubborn shake of her head. "I don't want to rest." Her meaning was clear.

Tigo's deep-set eyes glinted with a playful golden flame. "Then I can see to it that you don't get it."

The kiss was eagerness and heat on both sides. Tigo wound a hoard of her curls around his fist and commanded every move of her head as he subjected her to a rakish assault on her tongue. Sophia was just as needy; her hands ventured greedily beneath his coat, splaying across the fine material of his shirt. Awkwardly, yet beautifully, she straddled him until she almost had him flat on her desk.

"Soap." Tigo's body was definitely willing; his mind was faintly—very faintly—suggesting they take the fun elsewhere. "Babe?"

"Hmm…" Her tongue scoured every expanse of skin that she uncovered.

"Let me get you home."

"Tig—"

"My home," he clarified and kissed her smiling mouth.

The elevator opened in Tigo's sunken living room. He entered the space, carrying Sophia in his arms as they kissed wildly. Thoroughly involved in the kiss, Sophia kicked off her low-cut black leather boots and jacket. She desperately worked to undo her holster and broke the kiss momentarily to toss it on an armchair. It landed with barely a bounce. Then she was shucking off her blouse and the cami top beneath it.

"I'll take care of it," Tigo said near her ear and began a lazy suckle of the lobe.

Sophia honored his decision only to start helping him out of the loosened hunter-green tie and navy jacket. A ripple of arousal claimed her as she pushed the article of clothing from his very broad shoulders.

In no time, it seemed, Tigo was walking into his room and setting Sophia onto the middle of his bed. He made her sit long enough for him to relieve her of the blouse and cami as promised. Then he was expertly unhooking her bra for the second time that day.

With a nudge to her shoulder, he urged her to her back and caged her between his arms posted on either side of her. His smile had a subtle wolfish quality as he watched Sophia as if she were a confection he couldn't wait to devour.

He made himself comfortable at the joining of her thighs and cupped her breasts to molest her nipples beneath his thumbs.

Sophia pressed her head deeper into the fluffy pillows. She bit her lip, sensation abounding so much that she barely registered him relieving her of belt, slacks and underthings. He left no part of her untouched. His nose brushed the undersides of her breasts, nuzzling into the softly fragrant valley between. He folded his hands over her slender hips to stop their relentless squirm as she anticipated more of the slow, sensuous progression into lovemaking. He spared a few moments to favor her navel with a deep tonguing.

Sophia was still writhing from his sweet treatment of her belly button when his tongue probed her core. He applied the same breath-stealing treatment to her femininity that he had to her navel, albeit with more intensity.

She tried to say his name, but her voice was merely a silent breath. Sophia threaded her fingers through his hair. Suddenly he flipped her on her stomach to taste her back, gliding his tongue up her spine.

Sophia moaned her approval into the pillows, arching when his hands slipped beneath her. He massaged the petals of her sex with maddening slowness and then changed the exploration to include his middle fingers and thumbs. Her helpless cries, muffled into the pillows, stroked his ego and arousal simultaneously.

When he left her unexpectedly bereft of his touch, Sophia merely pleasured herself with its memory. She moved among the tangled bed coverings without shame, dwelling on the feel of his fingers inside her—his sleek muscular frame against her, sheltering her. She was scarcely coming down from her high when his hands returned to her hips to raise her slightly.

Tigo had disrobed and applied protection. He took her from behind in one smooth lengthy stroke. Sophia's response was immediate. She shuddered at the sensual intrusion, her breath trapped in her throat.

He kept her captive, deepening the penetration of his sex inside hers. Sophia bit into the pillow, which did little to stifle her cries. She moved with a bit more insistence, seeking her own peak of satisfaction.

Tigo was just as far gone. Sophia bit into the pillow again as his perfect teeth scraped her shoulder and he emitted his own approving groans. Clutching the wrinkled covers, he took her with increased fervor. Sophia climaxed first and wanted so much to melt afterward. Tigo wasn't done with her, though. He took his pleasure vigorously, but withdrew before he gave into release.

Sophia's long lashes moved rapidly as they shielded and unshielded her gaze. Santigo had turned her on her back; he reclaimed her a moment later. Deftly, he hooked one of her long legs across his shoulder. The increase of penetration was mind-blowing and she almost screamed her delight while raking her nails up and down his big thighs, two heavily chorded muscles.

They climaxed in unison that time. Tigo collapsed over Sophia. He recovered his breath long before she did.

"No," she protested when he moved. Regrettably, she had no strength to prevent him from shifting his weight.

Tigo only moved a few centimeters to slide his hand beneath one of the pillows along the headboard.

Sophia opened her eyes when she felt the pressure on her finger. Tigo had slipped on a silver band weighted with a square-cut diamond. Her eyes went wide and flew up to his face.

"Will you?" he asked.

She nodded eagerly against the pillow. "I will." She palmed the back of his head to draw him closer. "I will," she said once more before her mouth melded with his.

Chapter 15

Despite the fact that she was walking on air, Sophia stifled a sigh and grimaced when her assistant informed her that Officers Keele and Croft were waiting in her office. Sophia could tell by their eager expressions that their hard work had paid off. They'd found something; she was sure of it. They weren't going to like what she had to tell them one bit.

"Mornin', guys!" She greeted the younger officers in a voice that was sunny enough. It was hard not to be sunny given the fact that she finally had everything she wanted—*almost* everything. That would come once she became Mrs. Santigo Rodriguez.

Elzbeta's algae-green eyes had widened and were following every move of Sophia's left hand. "Ma'am? Are congrats in order?"

"Hmm?" Sophia inclined her head, stumped for a moment. Then she noticed where Elzbeta's gaze was focused. "Oh! Yes, yes, I guess they are!" She laughed at the unquestionable elation spicing her words.

Alvin sat slumped on the arm of the sofa, watching the women meet in the middle of the room for a quick hug. Then he was grinning, looking on as Elz took Sophia's hand for a closer inspection of the sparkling ring.

"Chief, you're taking the vows?" he teased, clapping when Sophia exhibited a playful curtsy. "Well, I hope we're about to make your day even better."

The hint of a cloud darkened Sophia's expression. "Yeah, guys, um…about that." She claimed the spot on the arm of the sofa Alvin had vacated and massaged her forearm through the sleeve of the V-neck lavender sweater she wore.

"You guys know about Harold Mackey," she began. The officers nodded. "I'm sure you can both understand that I don't want the same thing happening to either of you. Not when I'm the one who brought you into this."

"Chief." Elz clutched her hands. "I think I speak for both of us when I say how much we thank you for your concern. It's great to see that there are still some supervisors who care about a rookie's welfare instead of their disgrace." She looked down at her hands for several speculative seconds and then focused on Sophia again.

"But it's still like we said—we're vested in this. We want to see it to the end."

"I can't have you guys' blood on my hands, too." Sophia's expression was stubborn. "Harold was looking out for me in this thing, too. It's why he's dead—I know it."

"Chief." Alvin dug his hands into his khaki pockets. "We really think we're close to putting this whole thing to bed."

Still greatly reluctant, Sophia couldn't deny that her interest was piqued. "You've got my attention." She rested her arm along the back of the sofa.

The partners traded grins.

"We've got a new name to add to the mix," Alvin said. "Murray Dean."

"Say again?" Sophia felt her breathlessness return, but for an entirely different reason.

"Murray Dean," Elz obliged.

"How is that possible?" Sophia straightened. "You didn't get that from my notes." She couldn't have overlooked that name had it been there.

"That one came from another rookie we think may be caught up in this."

"I don't like this, guys." Sophia began to pace the spacious office. "There's too much sensitive info being shared among you all."

"They're scared, ma'am," Elzbeta explained, standing then, as well. "None of them signed up for this."

"I know." Sophia rested her chin in her palm and thanked God that the younger cops were still too green to go bad. "So who *is* this guy?" She hoped the query came across lightly enough.

"Nobody really knows." Elz shrugged. "Three of the guys swear they've seen him meeting with Sylvester Greenway's sons. Others say they've heard his name mentioned."

"And why would they think he was important?" Sophia wedged a thumbnail between her teeth.

"Apparently he's some kind of celebrity," Alvin shared. "Or he knows celebrities or something. Guess he's been on TV or one of those entertainment shows maybe."

"Right…"

"Ma'am?" Elz tilted her head at a curious angle. "You all right?"

"Murray Dean's an agent." Sophia massaged her temples and settled down in the nearest chair. "In fact, he's my sister's agent."

Sophia instructed Alvin and Elz to organize a meeting with their rookie colleagues and told them she'd be in touch. She spent the rest of the morning tracking down whatever suspicious information she could find on Murray Dean. She wasn't surprised that there was none to uncover. The man was spotless as he'd been years before when her father had forbidden Viva to put her career in his hands after she'd decided to put down stakes in California.

"You knew, Daddy. You knew it all along," Sophia mused.

Gerald Hail was the only one who hadn't fallen for Murray's easygoing, smooth-talking persona.

"What's he up to?" she whispered, tapping her fingers across the space bar on her desktop keyboard while staring at the home page of a well-known online entertainment magazine. Silently, she asked herself whether her sister knew.

Those thoughts were silenced by the arrival of Sophia's style team. For once, Sophia appreciated the intrusion.

"I see you dressed yourself," Lem noted, his brows creeping up higher to meet his nonexistent hairline.

"I think I did pretty good," Sophia argued.

"Lavender looks good on you, Sophia."

"Thank you, Kendra." Sophia stuck her tongue out at Lem.

"Mr. Rodriguez must be sharing a few of his impeccable style tips." Lem threw the barb and grinned when Sophia raised her hands to concede him the victory in the budding sparring match.

"Now let's get this thing started." Lem removed his beige leather jacket. "We've gotta help you pick out an outfit for the celebration party your mother organized."

"Are you kidding me?" Sophia leaned her head back on her desk chair and studied the recessed lights dotting her high ceiling. "I can't believe she still wants to go through with this thing."

"She's serious and very pleased that we're on hand to help you make the right selection." Lem looked toward the office door.

"Oh, boy," Sophia groaned when she saw the rack of evening gowns Freddy Donald pulled into the room.

* * *

Viva Hail never thought she'd yearn for the days when she could make a quick run to the drugstore in a pair of old sneakers, sweats and a faded T-shirt, hair unbound and face without the addition of dark glasses.

Now, it was sunglasses and scarves or risk being spotted and expected to spend a few hours signing autographs. Not that she minded...too much. Her fans were the best. Most had known her since her commercial days. She definitely appreciated them, but the success had not come without a price.

"Stop, Veev." She sighed, celebrating the fact that her trip to the deli down the block from Sophia's apartment had been uneventful. Her little sister had promised they'd have an early dinner, so Viva had decided to provide the fixings.

She knew Sophia too well not to recognize the little lilt of happiness when they'd spoken earlier. Sophia had rushed in, changed clothes and left for work before she had even turned over once. Viva could only hope the girl had taken her advice and that an announcement of the bridal variety was about to be made.

Viva was headed back into the soothing dim of the apartment lobby. She figured she could doff the subtle disguise and make it to the elevator. A hand closed on her arm just as she celebrated success.

With a bright, knowing smile in place, Viva prepared to meet the fan who'd noticed her.

What were the odds that it would be her very first fan? Blinking and unquestionably astonished, she found herself searching Rook Lourdess's jolting stare.

Thankfully Rook had the question Viva couldn't manage to ask.

"What are you doing here?" He spoke the words as if he was entranced; his eyes scanned every square inch of her face.

She ordered herself to snap out of it and tried to summon

words. "I…" *Speak, idiot!* "Sophia, I—I'm here for Sophie—The accident…"

Rook was moving close, vanquishing the distance separating them. Viva had to wonder if he even realized he was moving. The captivating gleam in his hypnotic eyes mingled with something she refused to chance a guess at.

She cleared her throat noisily and looked down. Gesture and movement caused Rook to snap out of his trancelike state.

"Thank you." Viva chanced looking up at him again. "For coming on board to look out for Sophie. I feel better knowing she's got the best."

A hint of a smile ghosted over his mouth, and his lone dimple flashed so fast it might have been imagined. "I feel better knowing you think I'm the best," he said.

"I always thought that." Viva's focus was resting on the powerful cords of his neck visible past the opening of the black shirt he wore over a stark white T-shirt. She focused on the sheer perfection of his face and wasn't surprised that she couldn't read his response to her admission.

It mattered little then, anyway, she thought, hearing one of Rook's men call out to him. He simply threw up a wave without turning to look at the man.

"How long are you here?" he asked her.

"Not sure."

Their gazes remained locked for a time. Viva roused first from the spell.

"I'll let you get back to your men," she said.

Of course he made no move to turn away from her. Viva realized she'd have to make that move. She inched past, trying not to touch him, but he was a master at invading space.

"Good to see you, Rook." She made a hasty escape into an opening elevator car.

Paula Starker twisted her swivel suede desk chair to and fro, biting her thumbnail as Alvin Keele left with his partner and seven first-year cops. When the door closed behind Alvin's back, Paula let her head fall back to the seat with a silent bump.

"Lord, can this get any messier?" she groaned. "Do you know how long Henry Fields has been an instructor at the academy?" She raised her hands defensively at the poisonous look Sophia threw her way. "So now what?"

"I want to know what he's got to say." Sophia tapped her fingers together while reclining in her chair in front of the desk. "Maybe he can lead us to who's at the top."

Paula took her turn at throwing off a poison-filled glare. "The man's even lower on the pole than Cole and Hertz."

"I don't care. It's worth it to at least talk to him."

"And what about Murray Dean? You think Viva knows anything?"

Sophia dropped the ankle that rested over her knee and scratched at her temple. "I hope not. My family's been through enough because of my and my sister's jobs."

Paula's champagne stare was sympathetic. "So what do you think Dean's connection is to Greenway?"

Sophia offered up a wry smile. "I'm pretty sure it's got nothing to do with construction."

Linus Brooks sat with a puzzled look on his dark angular face while observing one of his two best friends in the world. "You're sure she really said yes?" he asked for the second time. "She's really gonna marry *you?*"

Tigo relaxed on his office sofa, looking every bit the cat that swallowed the canary. "I assure you, Philadelphia's 'most finest' is going to be my wife."

Elias shrugged and looked over at Linus. "Guess even the 'most finest' among us has to experience bouts of brain loss every now and then."

"Congratulations, man. Seriously," Linus said once the office had quieted from the uproar of male laughter.

"It's about time," Eli said.

"Damn right it is." Tigo grinned.

"So when's the big day?" Linus asked.

"I'll get back to you on it." Tigo crossed his ankles on the coffee table. "I'm not gonna rush her. I can live off the fact that we've gotten *this* far a little while longer."

Eli beamed in an exaggerated fashion when he looked at Linus again. "Our baby's finally growing up, Line." Satisfied, he hooked both thumbs around the black suspenders he wore.

Linus chuckled, but he turned serious soon after. "We were worried…after her accident."

Tigo nodded. "Made me see what's really important. I want her for as long as we're meant to be. I won't worry about how long that is."

Satisfied as well, Linus unfolded his arms. "I agree, Eli. Our babe's definitely grown up." He stood.

The friends met in the center of the room for a group hug.

Sophia found her sister in high spirits when she got home that evening. Viva was floating about the house, setting out the feast she'd gotten from the deli that afternoon. She even had a fire going and Sophia's favorite bottle of wine chilling in a bucket on the center of the coffee table.

"Oh!" Viva gave a start when she walked into the living room. "I was hoping we'd have something to celebrate." She set napkins on the table.

"So what's Murray up to?" Sophia dropped her keys on the end table near the door.

"Murray?" Viva laughed shortly. "He's the same, I guess."

"That a good thing or bad?"

Viva propped her fists on her hips and studied her sister in bewilderment.

"His name came up in an investigation, Veev."

Viva let one hand drop. "He had something to do with your accident?"

Sophia sat on the arm of a chair. "Why would you think that?"

Viva shrugged, pushing her hands into the back pockets of her denim skirt. "You told me the accident had something to do with the investigation you're working on. I just assumed it was about that."

"Why do I get the feeling you were on your way home *before* my accident?"

Viva answered with an expression that confirmed the question.

"Talk to me, Veev."

"I don't have anything to say." Viva went to flex her fingers before the fire. "Not about that."

"Honey, are you involved in something you shouldn't be?"

"That's not it, Soph. I swear it." Viva whirled from the fireplace. "There are some things going on with Murray that have been setting me on edge lately."

"Is that why you came home?"

Wearily, Viva came to sit on the sofa, where she fidgeted with the plates and glasses set out for supper. "I think he knew I needed to leave. I've been asking questions about some of his new business associates. I could tell he didn't appreciate the nosiness."

Sophia slid off the arm of the chair down to the cushioned seat. "What kind of questions?"

Viva took a breath and eased forward to rest her elbows on her bare knees. "He's been hanging around a lot of cops. I know they were cops because I've heard him calling them Detective this and that…. He's as friendly with them as he is with folks I know to be drug dealers."

"Are you sure?" Sophia extended her hands inquisitively. "They could be cops, too—undercover."

"The movie biz is an intimate community, Soph." Viva smiled with wisdom beyond her thirty-six years. "Secrets always come to the surface, and if those folks are cops then this is really bad because I've seen more than a few of them dealing to my colleagues."

Sophia squeezed Tigo's arm to silently alert him to wait before moving away from the midnight-blue Yukon when he closed the passenger door once he'd helped her out.

That brisk afternoon, the Memorial Gardens Cemetery teemed with those en route to the graveside service for Sergeant Harold Mackey.

At her touch, Tigo moved directly before her. Sophia didn't think she'd ever been so grateful for the breadth of his chest; she took several breaths meant to usher in calm. No use. She was still as shaky as she'd been on awakening that morning.

Tigo pressed his face into the top of her head. "Do you want to do this?" He spoke into her hair.

"I have to."

"You don't *have* to do anything."

Sophia's smile was genuine but weak. "It's one of those figurehead responsibilities." She squeezed his hand to her cheek and looked up into the soothing depths of his eyes. "Stay close, please? Just because my presence is required doesn't mean I have to give sound bites and photo ops."

"You got it." Tigo graced her with a wink and then took note of the security detail. Rook Lourdess's men remained at a discreet yet workable distance should their skills be required before the end of the service.

Sophia didn't care about appearances that day. She kept her head on Tigo's shoulder as they moved closer to the site. Once there, she went to Harold's widow and grown children, who were there with their spouses and their own children. Harold's grandkids that he'd never see grow up, she thought. When she was tucked away in Tigo's hold again, they headed for their seats.

"Someone's going to pay for this," she muttered. "Harold was a good cop. I'll prove it."

"How's his wife doing?" Tigo asked.

Sophia's gray gaze glistened with unshed tears as she studied the family. "The kids are all very successful, and they're good kids. Their mother won't want for anything."

Sophia never once released Tigo's hand. Silently, he admitted that he liked the way she held on to it. Once seated, Sophia kept the hand captive in her lap.

"You're coming home with me afterward. Hope Viva won't mind."

"We could use the space anyway."

Tigo caught the tightness in her voice, but he thought it best not to inquire. "Does it look like it played out the way they said?" he asked of Harold Mackey's demise instead.

"It looks that way." Sophia gritted her teeth. "But I know Harold too well for things to be what they appeared. No way would he have told me about that money if he and Ernest Lyman were gonna run off with it."

Tigo smoothed his thumb across the back of her hand. "Have you told anyone else about it?"

Sophia smirked. "I'm pretty sure they know. They always know...."

The day beamed with sun although the air held a definite chill. After a while, Sophia held Tigo's hand for warmth as well as support. She only let go to brush tears from her lashes. The pastor's words, as he eulogized Harold, affected everyone's emotions.

"I hope this wasn't too soon for you?"

Funeral attendees milled about the yard following the interment. Sophia thanked Elias and Clarissa for being there.

Clarissa hugged Sophia, who had finally let go of Tigo's hand to greet them. "We wanted to be here," she said, smiling as the cold wind whipped her hair around her lovely face.

"But thank you." Clarissa's expression was unmistakably melancholy as she thought of her late aunt.

"What are you doing after this?" Elias asked Tigo while the women embraced.

"Kicking back for the rest of the day…I guess." Tigo saw that Sophia had pulled back from Clarissa to answer her phone. He stepped to his fiancée; exchanging looks with Elias and Clarissa when they all heard Sophia's hushed "What?"

Glancing around the grounds, Tigo saw that many of the city officials in attendance appeared to be rushing for their cars, which were parked around the long circular drive.

Santigo, Elias and Clarissa didn't have to wait long to find out what had caused the commotion.

Sophia eased her phone into a side pocket on her dark dress. "Judge Oswald Stowe was just found in his chambers. They say it was suicide."

Chapter 16

Sophia shook her head at the sound of Paula's laughter as they spoke by phone the next morning. By then, the news about the fallen judge had spread citywide. While the media speculated about the cause, city officials worked hard at damage control. It was something that had become the norm as of late.

"Cole's practically begging to tell me everything he knows," Paula said. "Whether there's a deal on the table or not." She laughed wickedly. "The rats are definitely running for cover."

"Have you talked to him about it?" Sophia switched her mobile to the other ear while quickening the pace of her steps.

"I told him I'd be in touch once I checked on your schedule. It's only right that you be there, girl."

"I'm just ready to put the whole damn thing to bed." News of Cole's withering resolve was not as sweet for Sophia as it should have been.

"Hang in there. We're close. I can feel it." Paula sighed.

"Just remember Cole's no fool." Sophia pulled open the front doors to the precinct. "He won't just spill his best secrets for nothing."

"True, but he knows the first to talk gets the best deal."

"Pauly—"

"Don't worry, don't worry. I'm not letting him skate. He's gonna do serious time, but I may be willing to…encourage the judge to be lenient. He's not walkin' away from this. None of them are."

"Okay." Sophia hoped she sounded convinced. "All right then, I'll talk to you later." She wrapped up the call with the D.A. just as she approached the switchboard station.

Sophia caught sight of Kelly Fields across the expansive office area. She waited for the girl to finish up the conversation she carried on with two coworkers, then waved to get her attention.

The young woman had to be going through a lot with her father, Henry Fields, under suspicion following the allegations made by the rookie cops who had once been under his instruction. Still, Kelly put on a welcoming smile as she closed the distance to Sophia.

"Chief." She extended both her hands for a shake.

Sophia obliged. "How are you holdin' up?"

"It's hard." Kelly smiled thinly. "Half the folks I work with think I only have this job because of my father. I'm sure they're eating this up," she added in a softer voice.

Sophia rubbed Kelly's sweater sleeve. "Just try to remember you haven't done anything wrong."

Kelly nodded. "That's what Alvin said."

"He's right." Sophia dipped her head to bring her eyes level with Kelly, and she smiled at the advice given by her boyfriend, Alvin Keele.

"It's gonna work out, Kelly. Just let your dad know you're there for him. The rest'll take care of itself."

Again, Kelly nodded, her smile coming through easier that time. "And *that's* exactly what Mr. J said."

"Mr. J?"

Kelly laughed, a happy light thriving in her gaze. "Sorry, I meant Detective Eames. I've called him Mr. J since I was a kid."

Sophia smiled. "Well Mr. J's right, and he's a good guy to have in your corner."

"Oh, I know." Kelly hugged herself. "And he wouldn't be any place else. He and Daddy go way back. All the way back to the academy."

Sophia eased her hands into the side pockets of her straight black skirt. "They went to the academy together?" She wanted to silence the voice of cop suspicion that suddenly gnawed at the rim of her conscience.

Kelly gave a nod. "Yep. All the way through. He and Daddy have been close for years. That's why I called him last week. I wanted to know if he could help Daddy through any of this."

"So you told Jofi Eames about the allegations?"

"Well, I figured he knew, anyway, but he did sound strange when I buzzed him upstairs to talk." Kelly shook her head. "I felt like a heel for bothering him, especially after I saw the news that night."

"The news?" Sophia prayed Kelly wouldn't grow suspicious over her repetition of the questions, but tension was suddenly hitting her out of nowhere. But then…what hadn't lately? She had really only stopped by to see how Kelly was doing. The young woman had been so sweet to her back when everyone else was treating her like an outcast.

"Yeah…" Kelly tapped her fingers on her chin, still not taking issue with Sophia's keen interest. "The day I called was the day all that happened with Sergeant Mackey down at the garage."

Sophia had to sit then in one of the chairs along the wall

just inside the switchboard office. Kelly's call couldn't have been the same one Jofi had gotten from the switchboard. The anonymous "tip" that had sent him rushing to stop Harold Mackey from running off with money from the Greenway Construction truck that was doubling as transpo for money laundering. It was a coincidence, wasn't it?

"Chief?" Kelly eased down in the chair next to Sophia. "You okay?"

Blinking rapidly, Sophia nodded.

"Sophia?" Kelly patted her knee.

"I'm good, Kelly, thanks." Sophia forced a weak smile. "Not enough sleep last night."

Kelly patted her knee again. "Our coffee down here is amazing. I'll go fix you a cup."

Once Kelly had bustled off, Sophia let her forehead drop into her palm.

Somehow, Sophia was able to put the revealing and unexpected conversation with Kelly Fields into perspective. She tried to make sense of it, tried to make it fit into the current state of things. There was really nothing to it except a lot of speculation on *her* part, she admitted. "Circumstantial at best" was what Paula would probably say.

However, in the days following the chat with Kelly, Sophia discovered that she wasn't the only cop with a more suspicious than normal streak.

Sophia would never admit to her mother how much the celebration party helped. It felt good to have a little fun, dance a little, nibble on a few exquisite treats. There was that as well as the fact that the celebration party served a dual purpose.

Once Sophia had accepted Tigo's proposal, Gerald and Veronica Hail wasted no time turning their daughter's job celebration into an engagement party.

Santigo Rodriguez arrived at the Hails' beautiful home

with a lovely woman on each arm—his fiancée and his mother. Dr. Della Sanford Rodriguez beamed almost as brightly as the bride to be. The university professor was so thrilled about the hoped-for union that she'd insisted on giving the soon-to-be newlyweds a lavish reception once the wedding date was set.

"So many people here tonight," Della marveled, her vivid hazel eyes sparkling with excitement and a smidge of cunning. "It'd be nice if you two eased everyone's curiosity and gave us a wedding date."

Over Della's head of short, glossy curls, Santigo and Sophia shared knowing looks and laughter. Tigo leaned down to brush a kiss across his mother's flawless molasses-dark cheek.

"You're the only curious one, Ma."

"Not possible," Della argued as Sophia kissed her cheek next.

Paula was first to greet the trio upon their arrival. She hugged Della and reconfirmed her commitment and excitement about speaking with the woman's students when she visited the university the following month as a guest lecturer.

"Do you two mind if I steal away the chief for a minute?"

"Dance with me, Professor?" Tigo offered an elbow to his mother and whisked her away.

"Are you sure about this?" Paula propped a hand on her hip.

Sophia frowned. "I've always wanted to marry Tig."

Paula turned on her friend, eyes flashing as brightly as her gown. She took Sophia's elbow and pulled her off to a hidden corner in the foyer.

"Are you serious about this thing tonight? It's not your job to be on the front lines anymore, remember? You've done enough. Let the rest put in work for a change."

"I'm still a cop, Pauly." Sophia folded her arms across the

bodice of her plum-colored satin-under-chiffon gown. "See-ing it through to the end, remember?"

"It is the end," Paula boasted. "All our little birds are chirping merrily."

"All but one."

"So—"

"Come and get a drink with me." Sophia linked arms with Paula and tugged her into the brightly lit, conversation-filled room.

Viva Hail debated returning to the bar for another drink to calm her nerves. As if another would help any more than the first two she'd had. She told herself that Sophia was right. Someone had to make the first move.

And if they didn't accept? Well, then…at least she could say that she tried.

Viva was so caught up in her doubts and anticipations that she didn't realize her uncertain steps had carried her directly to the people she'd debated approaching.

Veronica Hail saw her eldest child first and stopped mid-sentence while speaking with her husband and another couple.

Gerald cupped his wife's elbow, his eyes narrowed in concern. "Baby?" He followed the line of her gaze. "Viva?"

Viva opened her mouth to share the speech she'd rehearsed. She never had the chance to utter a word. Gerald and Veronica brushed past the couple they'd been talking to and pulled their daughter into a crushing hug.

Across the room, Sophia gasped upon witnessing the scene between her family.

"Like that?" Tigo murmured. He referred to the attention he was giving to the spot behind Sophia's ear.

"Yeah…" Sophia was undeniably affected by the man

who held her, yet almost equally so by what she'd witnessed between her parents and sister.

Tigo moved back to judge her expression. He turned to see what had her so entranced and observed the mini-reunion between his soon-to-be in-laws. "It's about damn time." He grinned and turned back to nuzzle behind his fiancée's ear.

The engaged couple had been snuggled in one remote corner or another throughout the course of the evening. No one begrudged them for it. Everyone in attendance agreed that it was about damn time.

A vibration between the betrothed signaled that someone's phone was ringing. It was Sophia's. Minutes into her cryptic conversation, Tigo was frowning with violent intent.

"I think it's a very fitting place," Sophia told the caller. "If you want to hear what I have to say, you'll be there....No, no, we won't be bothered." She looked around at the room of happy faces.

"Everyone's here at the party," she said, wincing when the connection severed abruptly in her ear. She winced again at the murderous look on Tigo's striking face.

"Do you know what the hell it is you're doing?"

She tugged the lapel of his tuxedo jacket. Bringing him close, she touched her lips to his and murmured, "Trust me."

With the exception of late-night security staff, city hall was a virtual ghost town. Corridors teaming with bodies by day seemed as remote as a desert isle by night.

Sophia wasn't surprised to find that she wasn't the first to arrive. She clicked on a lamp to bathe her office in golden light. "Thanks for not making me wait," she said.

Detective Jofi Eames languished behind the desk. "Lookin' good, Chief." He eyed her gown. "The bravery's impressive, too. Must be the new title."

"Doubt it. I'm only a figurehead." She strolled into the room. "Henry Fields labeled you as his contact. Did you turn him or was it the other way around? Maybe things went south when he asked you to approach Mike Cana about bringing Alvin Keele into your mess. All that diabolical planning, and for what?"

"Henry and me go way back," Jofi spat. "He wanted his kid's boyfriend to have a piece of the pie, something more to offer Kelly than a cop's salary. It's what friends do. They look out for each other." He leered. "But you wouldn't under-stand that since you don't have any friends. No one to have your back, do you favors."

Sophia smiled. "So I guess that means you approached Henry first?"

Jofi's cool expression showed traces of wear then.

"You shouldn't have involved his daughter." Her smile broadened when she saw him blink. "Oh, right. I guess you didn't think I'd put it together with Kelly, either." She crossed her arms over her chest.

"What was that you said about me not making friends? Actually, Kelly's someone I know and like a lot. Her call was your so-called 'tip,' wasn't it? In case somebody checked up behind you, they'd know a call came in at that time, but they wouldn't know what it was about. You'd be free to create any story you wanted."

"Toy cop." Jofi's voice was like iron as he pushed up from the desk. "Who are you to question me? You're right, you know? That promotion of yours was just for show. It could've been mine if I'd wanted it."

"And would Murray Dean still be pulling the strings?" She shrugged. "How does he fit into all this?"

The faint traces of wear began to shine through more po-tently on Jofi's face. "Why don't you just focus on decorat-ing your fancy office and smiling pretty for the cameras?" He sneered. "This is too big for you, Detective."

"Thanks for remembering that I'm still a cop, Jofi."

"Think about that—*a* cop." He leaned back to study her

smugly. "One lone cop. You don't know anyone. Never took time—usually off working on your own. Doin' the partner thing only when you *have* to."

He rounded the desk. "This job is about friends, *Detective.* Friends, connections—one hand washing the other. You're all alone here, Sophia." His hand went to the holster at his hip. "You should've been smart enough to back off when I drove that truck into your car and smart enough to know your digging would get you in trouble one day."

"And *you* should've been smart enough to know that good cops have friends, too."

"And that they don't have to buy their friends. They earn 'em."

Two voices called out from the shadowed forest of corridors beyond the office door. Jofi's hand froze on the weapon he was about to release. There was movement in the shadows. Jofi appeared stricken by the sight of his colleagues— some familiar, others not so much. All were decked out in evening attire.

"Guest of honor leaves her own party, it's the guests' duty to follow," Captain Roy Poltice called out.

"It'd be a good idea for you to take your hand off the weapon, sir." Officer Alvin Keele moved in—gun aimed and steady as he swept the room with three other officers. "All right there, Chief?" he called to Sophia, never taking his eyes from Jofi.

"Just fine." She kept her eyes on her longtime colleague, as well. Inwardly, she sighed with relief that her insane plan to shame Jofi before the people he had disgraced had worked.

Jofi grinned toward Alvin. "You gonna arrest me, kid?"

"Right now, we just have a few more questions about the Harold Mackey shooting," Captain Poltice said. "We'll go on from there."

"You'll know when an arrest is pending," Sophia added.

"You don't have crap on me."

"D.A.'s not so sure about that, Jofi." Sophia put her hands on her hips. "Especially after her chat with several rookie cops."

Jofi's Adam's apple bobbed in an exaggerated manner as he swallowed hard.

"Looks like you and Henry Fields were wrong about them," Poltice said. "This new breed of cops is coming to *work* for their pay—not to steal it."

With uniformed officers on either side of him, Jofi knew better than to resist, but that didn't stop him from snarling at his colleagues. "Fools! Believing in some snot-nosed first-year punks over *me?* My rep's gonna have you for breakfast before you get out of that fancy tux, Cap!"

"Don't count on it," yet another voice called from the crowd.

There was a murmur of surprise when Deputy Commissioner Tevin Deese stepped in from the shadows.

"Last night your associate Waymon Cole sold everybody out from himself and Hertz all the way up to the top—including your buddy Murray Dean." Deese's angular face appeared like granite.

"Right now, Meeks and Franklin are too busy trying to figure out a way to save their own asses. Your buddy Hertz folded like a fifty-cent towel when we questioned him—gave you up fast and neat."

At last, Jofi appeared too stricken to say anything.

"Get him out of here," Deese growled to the officers.

The detective bowed his head as he was led through the corridor of plainclothes and uniformed cops of all ranks and levels of administration. There were even members of the Internal Affairs Division on hand.

A wave of silence blanketed the hall and office as Jofi's escorts led him from the area. Sophia, still as a statue, gave into the weariness that she'd struggled to suppress while confronting Jofi. Then her ears picked up the sound of—

She shook her head, believing the weariness had her hearing things. Gradually though, the sound heightened and Sophia recognized it as applause. Everyone was clapping. Some cheered, while others whistled. Sophia brought a hand to her mouth and discovered she was smiling and then laughing. She joined in the applause and cheered for her colleagues and for the trust they'd put in her that night.

The hall gradually cleared. The pace quickened when Sophia informed her coworkers that the party was far from over and that there was plenty of food left. Almost everyone had made a point of approaching her on their way out, personally thanking her for uncovering the scandal and for being brave enough to go it alone when everyone else was giving her their ass to kiss.

The well-wishers rounded out with two directors from the Internal Affairs Division, who told Sophia how much they looked forward to working with her in her new capacity as chief of detectives.

"You keep up *this* kind of track record and you're gonna put us out of business," Leland Fines told Sophia.

"I'll say," Beverly Silver agreed. "You ever get tired of what you're doing, you've got an office on our end."

"Would you people quit trying to steal all the best folks for yourselves?" Captain Poltice approached to scold the directors.

Fines and Silver took it all in stride.

"See you guys back at the party," Fines said and then escorted his colleague out the office.

"Sneaky buzzards." Poltice grinned and then turned to extend a hand to Sophia. "Thank you, Chief. You know, you may've started something tonight—ushered in a new era of pride in the job for the uniform."

"And here I thought I was just a figurehead."

Poltice grimaced at the comparison. "You were supposed

to be," he admitted. "Something pretty on top to keep everyone's eyes on you instead of the corrosion underneath. Ironically, keeping our eyes on you is what finally opened them." He shook his head and smiled encouragingly. "You keep right on doing what you're doing." He grinned past her shoulder and nodded. "You can start with taking care of *this* guy."

Sophia turned and found herself looking up into Tigo's stony face.

"You okay?" She brought her hands up to his face.

"You should be asking *us* that." Detective Burt Morgan sighed. "This man's almost impossible to hold down. Here's hopin' we never have to arrest him."

"We thought we were gonna have to sit on him when Jof went for that gun," Detective Calvin Daniels added.

Sophia laughed. "Thanks, guys. I'll take it from here."

Tigo jerked his fiancée into a fierce hug before she could say another word.

"It's all right, shh… I'm okay." She cooed the words until his embrace almost stifled her breath.

"I asked that fool to look out for you, damn it." Tigo hid his face in her neck. He squeezed her even tighter. "He helped to set up those kids, didn't he?"

"Shh…" Sophia sprinkled kisses on his cheek, mouth and jaw. "It's over now. I'm okay and everything's fine."

Tigo moved back, brown eyes sparkling with mixed amounts of relief and disbelief. "*You're* fine, but you didn't think to ask if *I'd* be." He pulled her close again. "I love you."

"I love you back." She sighed.

"I think I'll let you handle all the legal issues from this point out. Deal?"

"Ha! Deal… Only, I may need your help with one more thing."

He looked down into her eyes, passion, love, devotion all brimming in the pitch depths. "Name it."

"I need you to help me find Reggie."

Tigo smiled at the mention of his friend Judge Reginald Creedy. "Something with the case?" he asked.

Sophia gave a half shrug. "Not about the case." She clasped her hands over his chest and stared at her engagement ring. "I think it's time to make us legal. What do you say to that?"

Tigo's ebony gaze narrowed, his smile emerging. "Well, I've already got the tux so…" He propped her chin on his fist. "Absolutely, Chief."

Moments later, his lips met hers.

* * * * *

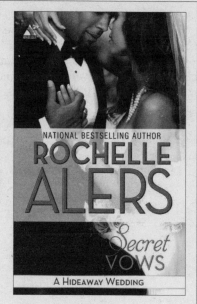

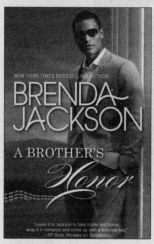

REQUEST YOUR FREE BOOKS!

2 FREE NOVELS
PLUS 2 FREE GIFTS!

KIMANI ROMANCE™

Love's ultimate destination!

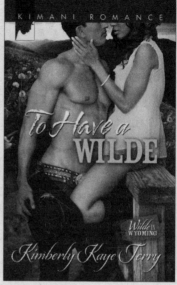

Just when he thought he'd never find love…

KIMANI ROMANCE

Perfect Match

DARA GIRARD

Out of desperation, Hannah Olaniyi takes on a seemingly unwinnable case. And her new client, Amal Harper, is testing her in ways she never imagined. As tempers ignite over conflicting strategies, Hannah fights a desire that's becoming all-consuming—and very distracting! But is it too late for Amal to mend his bad-boy ways and claim his future with Hannah?

HARLEQUIN®
www.Harlequin.com

Available July 2013 wherever books are sold!

KPDG3140713